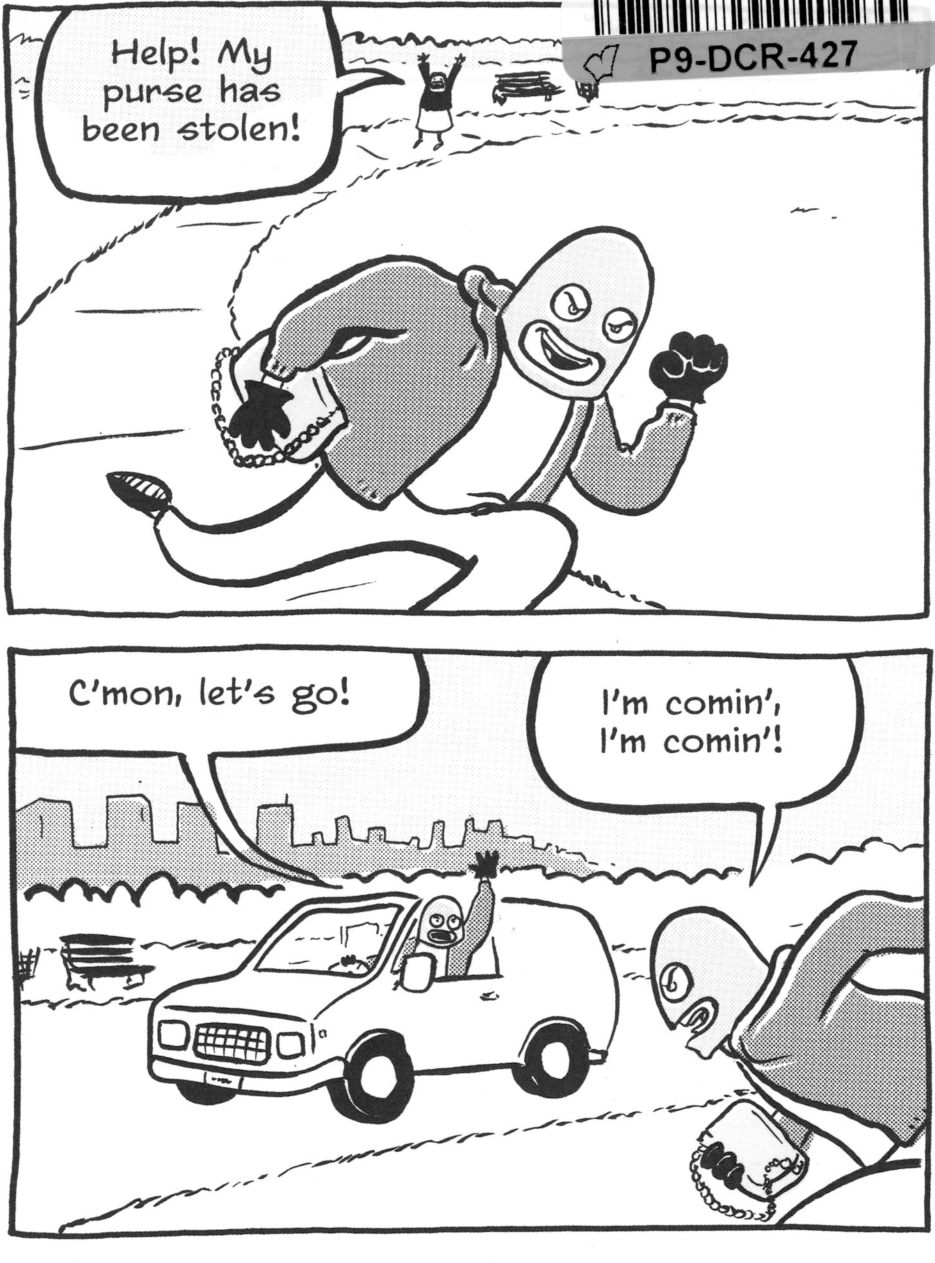
Help! My purse has been stolen!
C'mon, let's go!
I'm comin', I'm comin'!

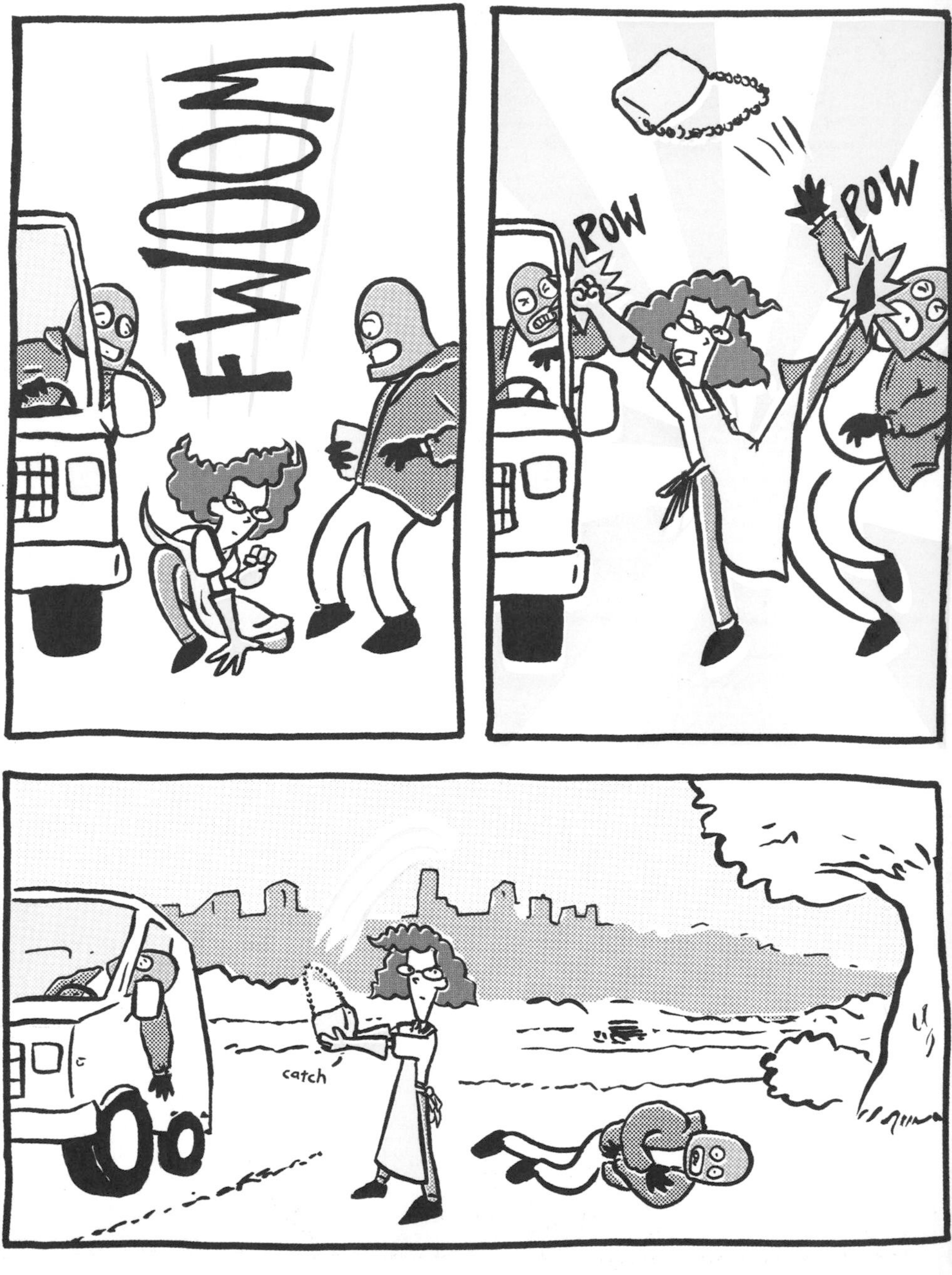
FWOOM
POW
POW
catch

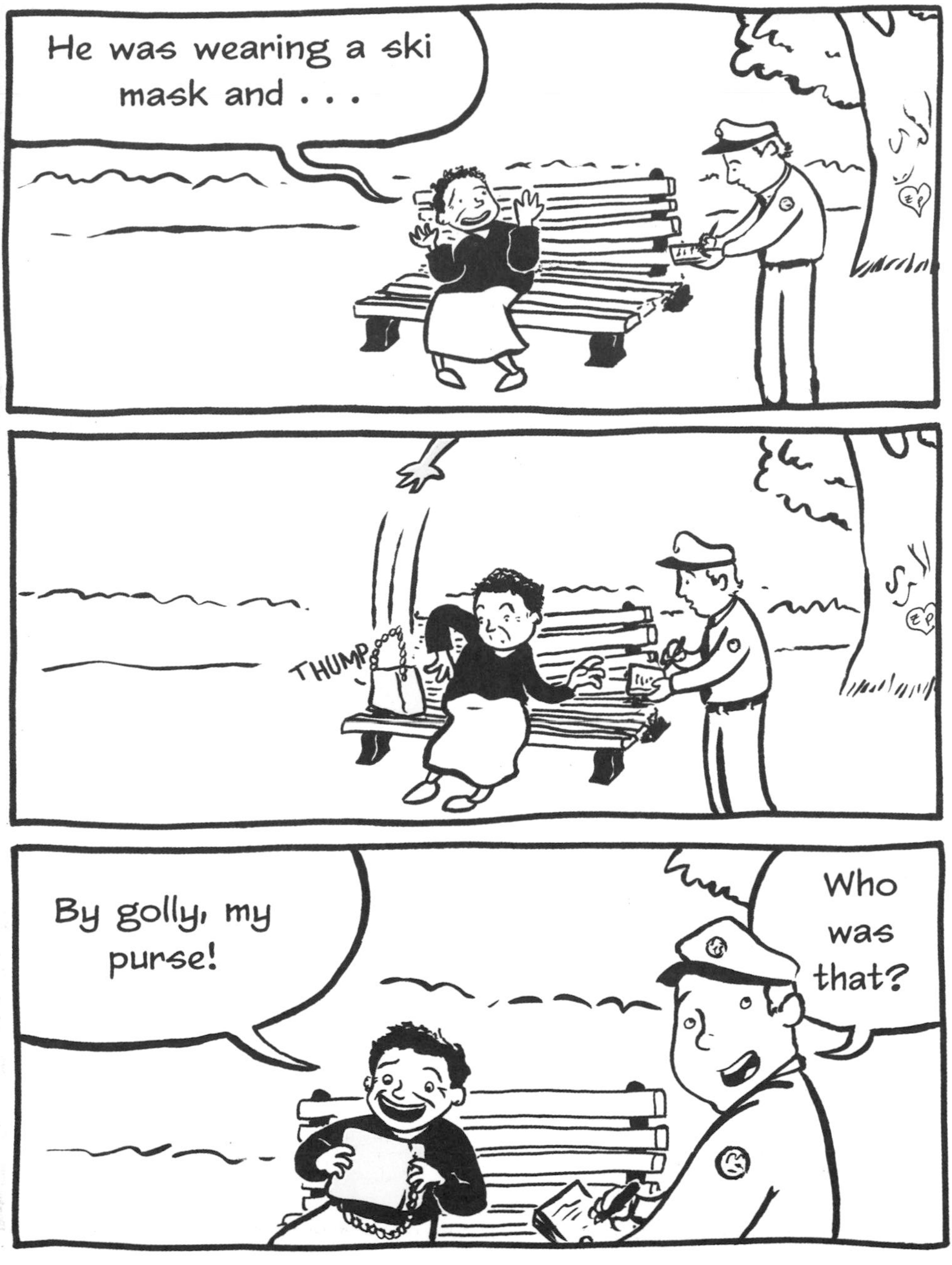
He was wearing a ski mask and . . .
THUMP
By golly, my purse!
Who was that?

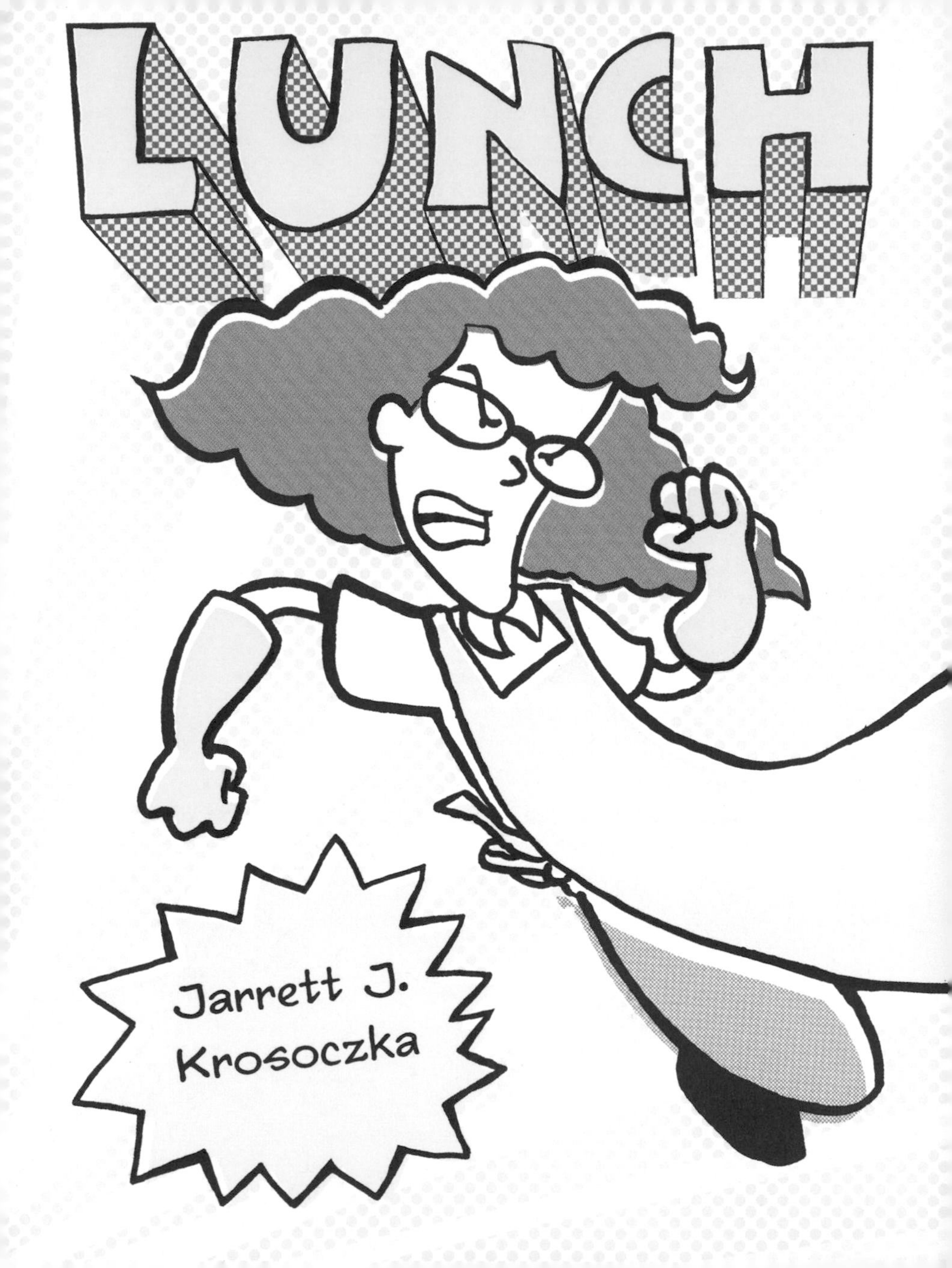
LUNCH
Jarrett J.
Krosoczka

LADY

and the League of Librarians

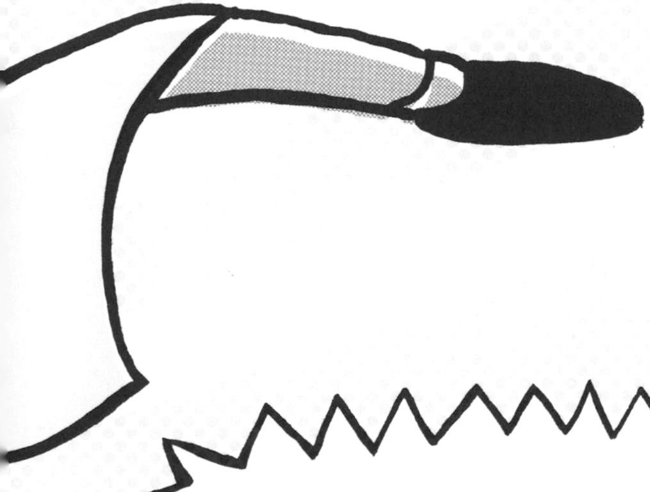

Alfred A. Knopf New York

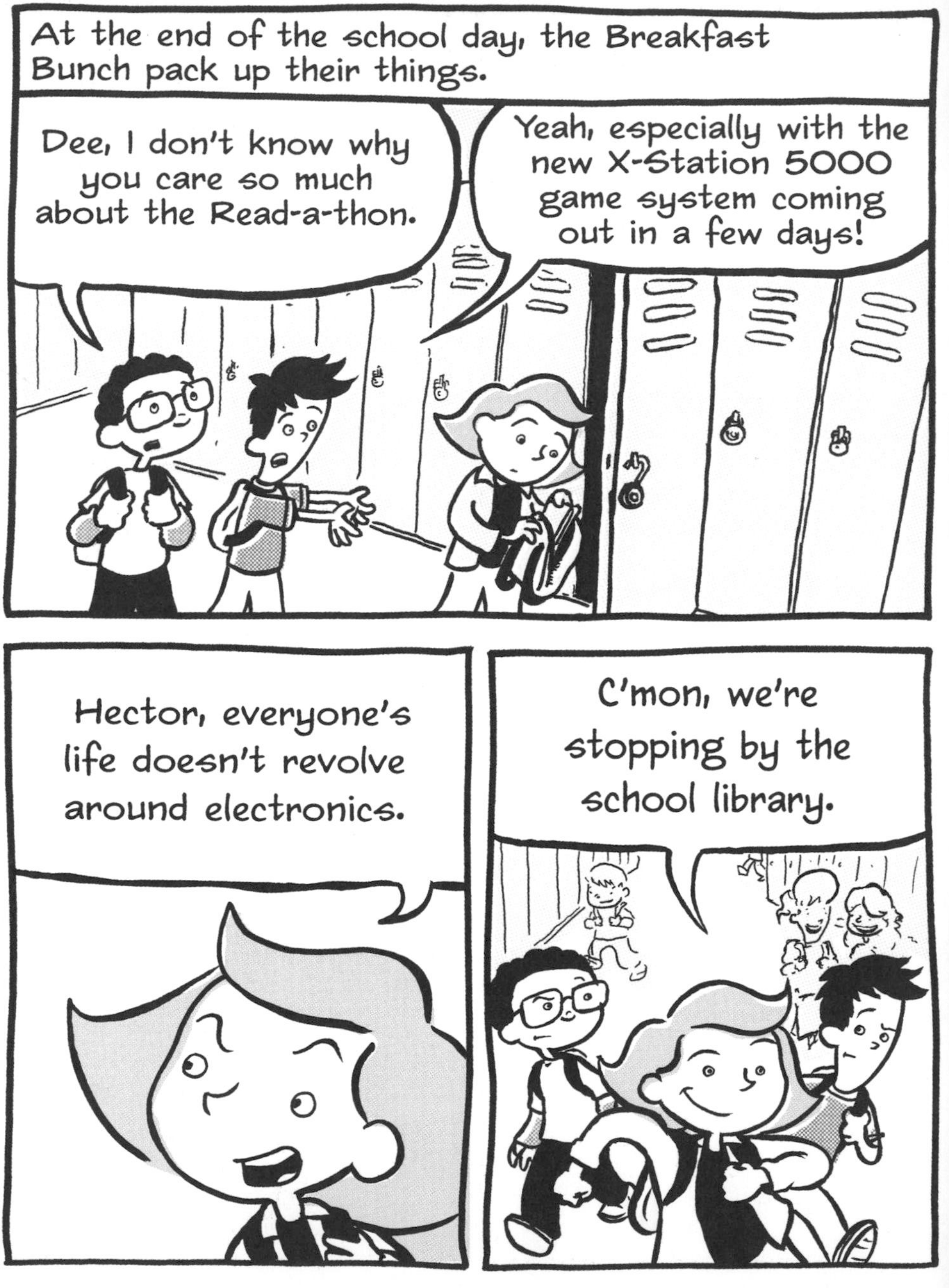
At the end of the school day, the Breakfast Bunch pack up their things.
Dee, I don't know why you care so much about the Read-a-thon.
Yeah, especially with the new X-Station 5000 game system coming out in a few days!
Hector, everyone's life doesn't revolve around electronics.
C'mon, we're stopping by the school library.

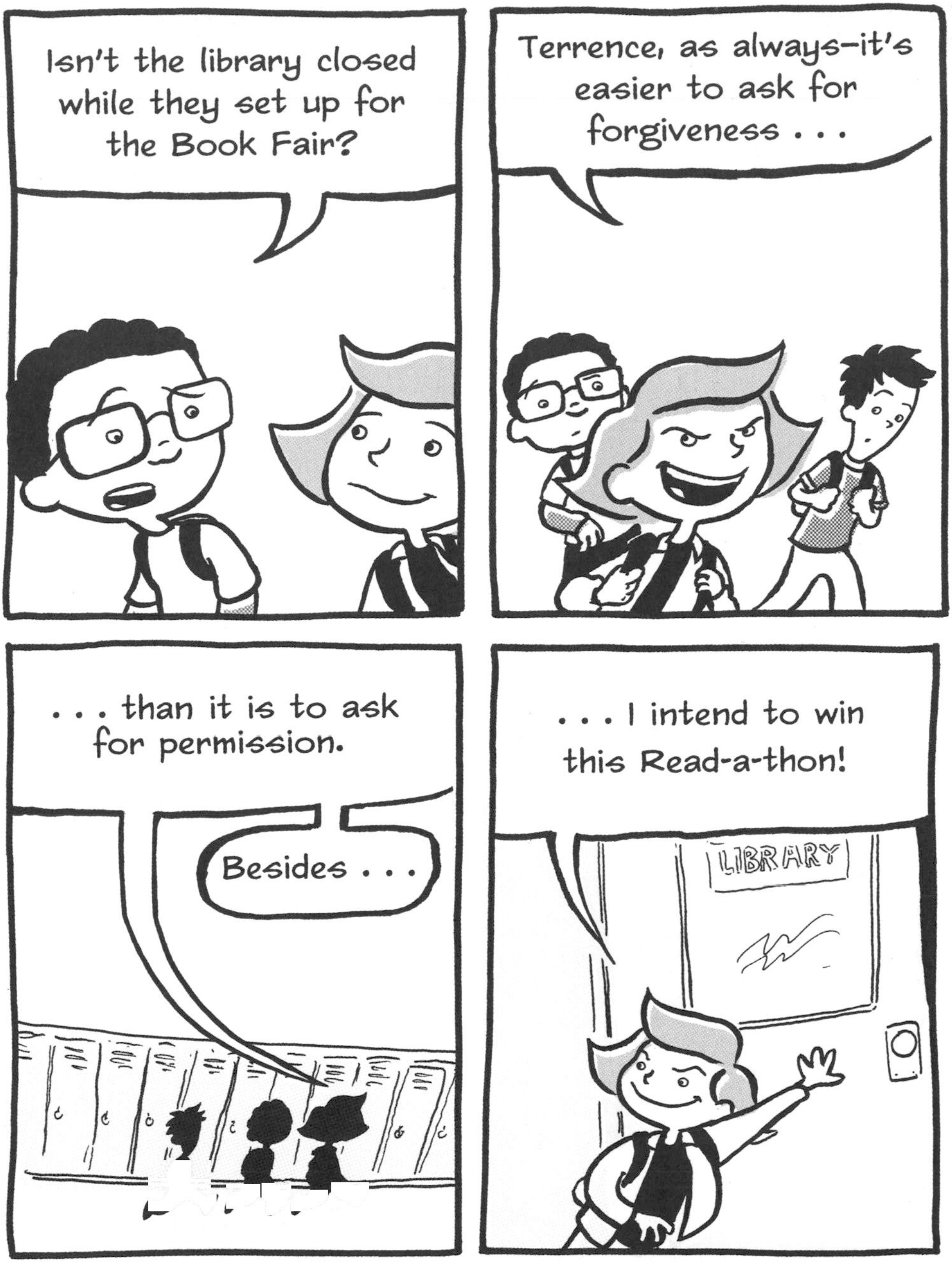
Isn't the library closed while they set up for the Book Fair?
Terrence, as always—it's easier to ask for forgiveness . . .
. . . than it is to ask for permission.
Besides . . .
. . . I intend to win this Read-a-thon!
LIBRARY

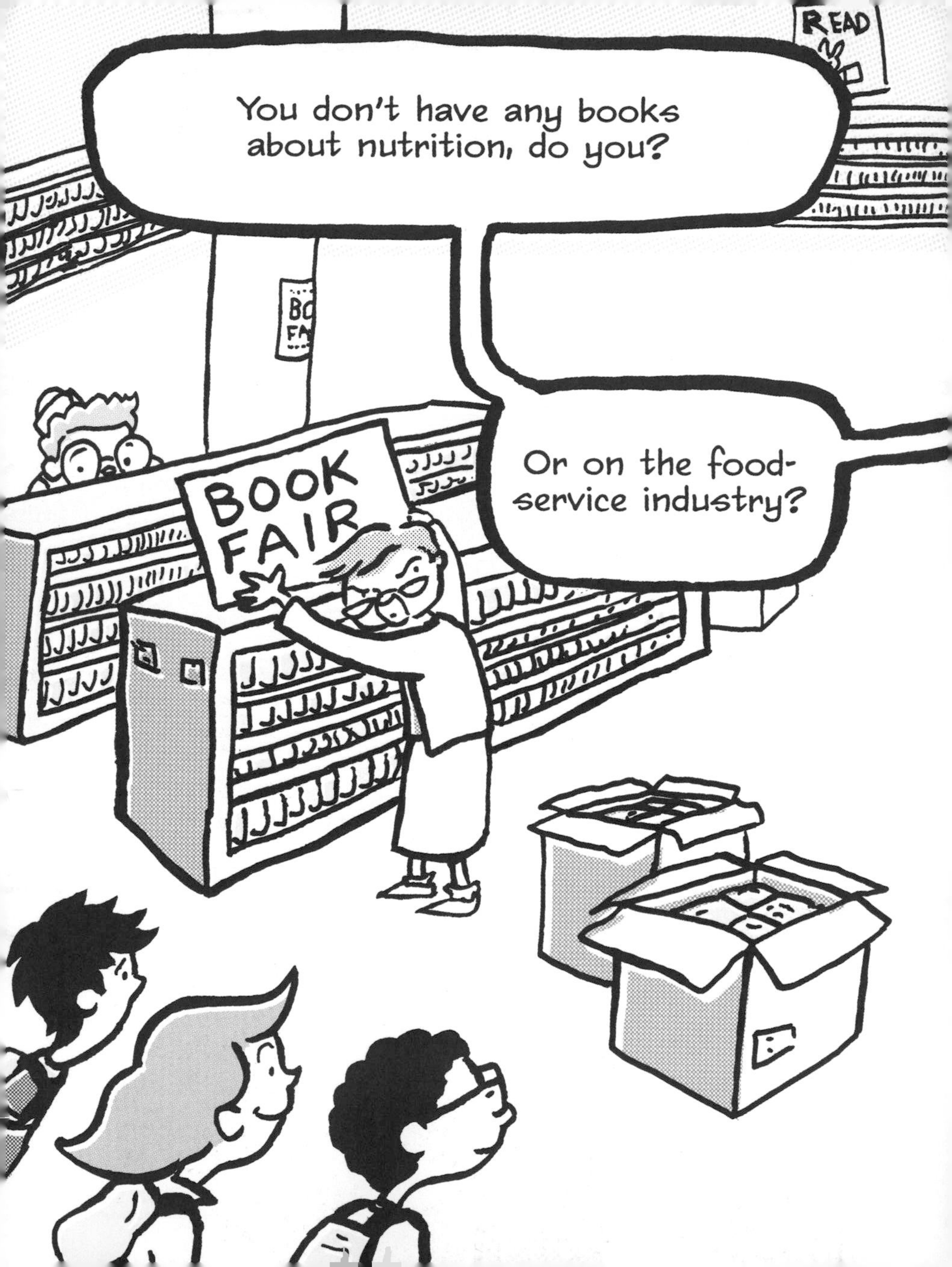
READ
You don't have any books about nutrition, do you?
BOOK FAIR
Or on the food-service industry?

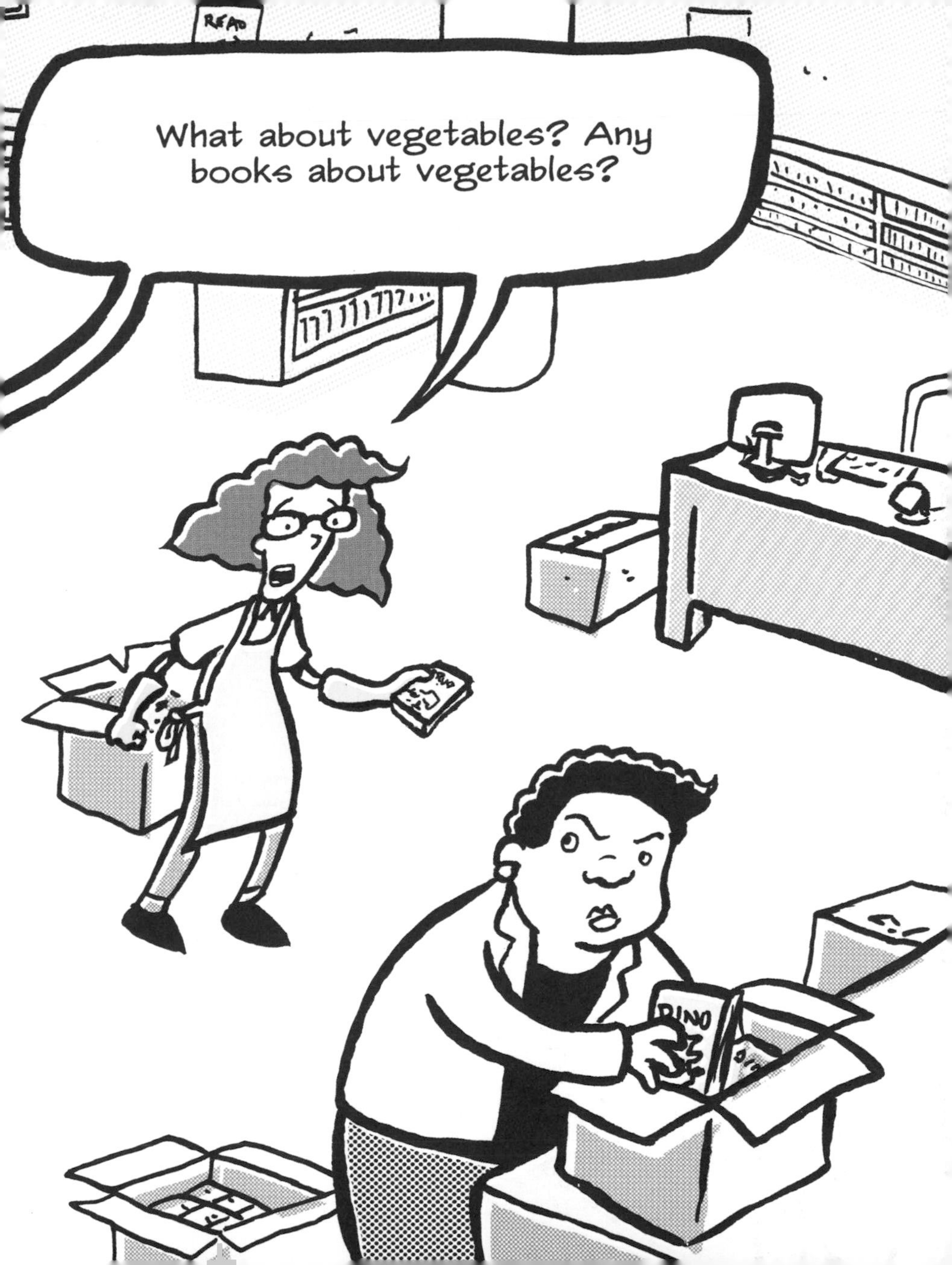
What about vegetables? Any books about vegetables?
READ
DINO

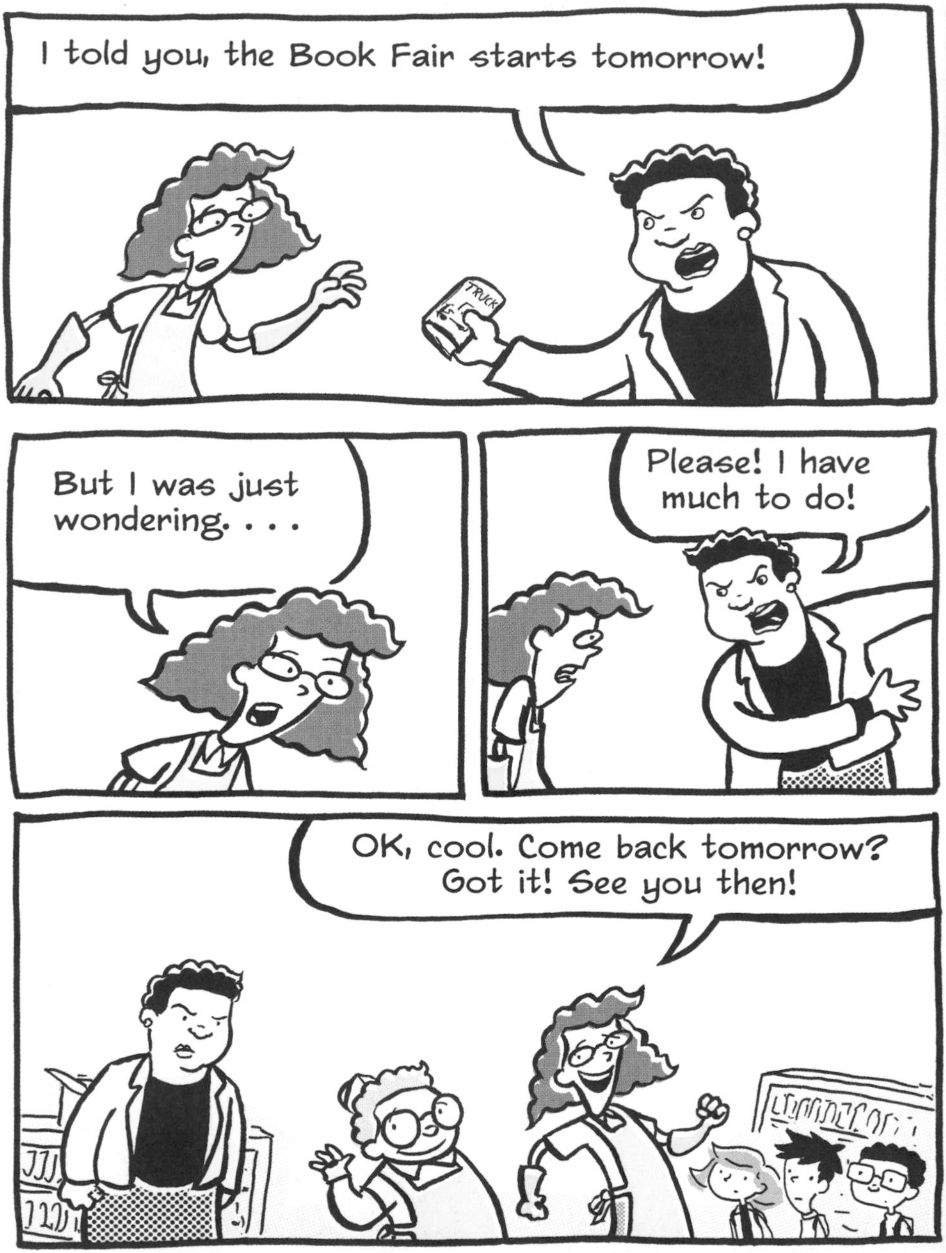
I told you, the Book Fair starts tomorrow!
TRUCK
But I was just wondering. . . .
Please! I have much to do!
OK, cool. Come back tomorrow? Got it! See you then!

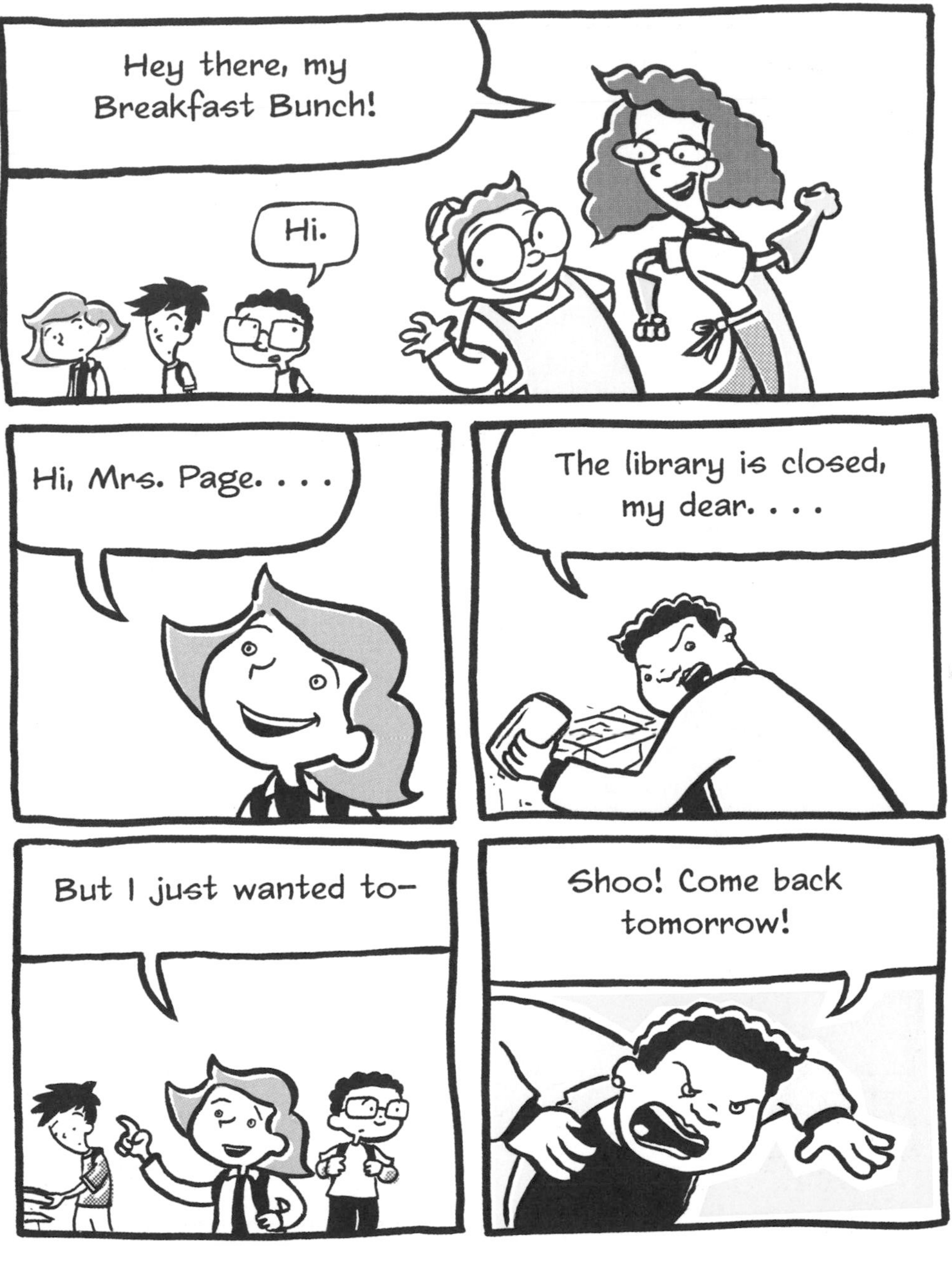
Hey there, my Breakfast Bunch!
Hi.
Hi, Mrs. Page. . . .
The library is closed, my dear. . . .
But I just wanted to–
Shoo! Come back tomorrow!

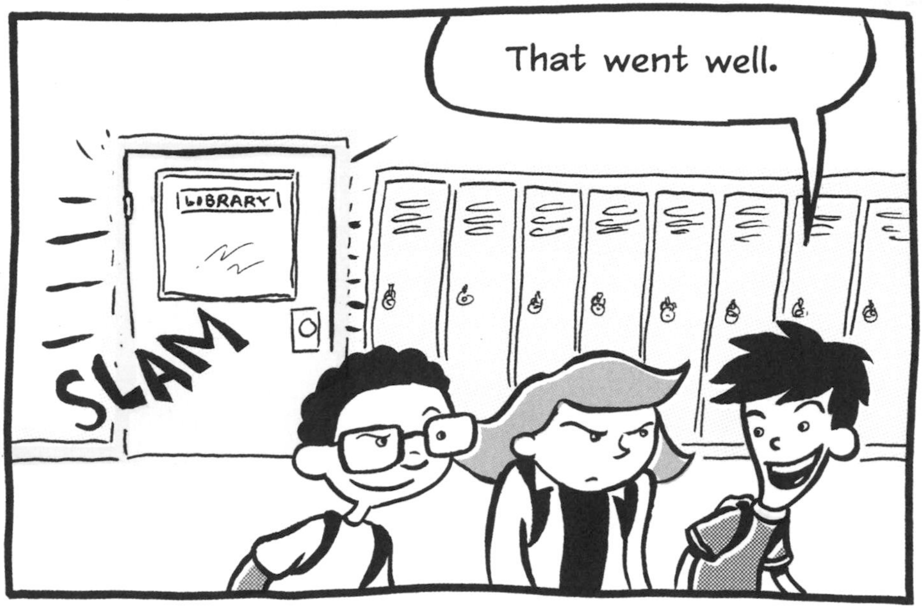
That went well.
LIBRARY
SLAM

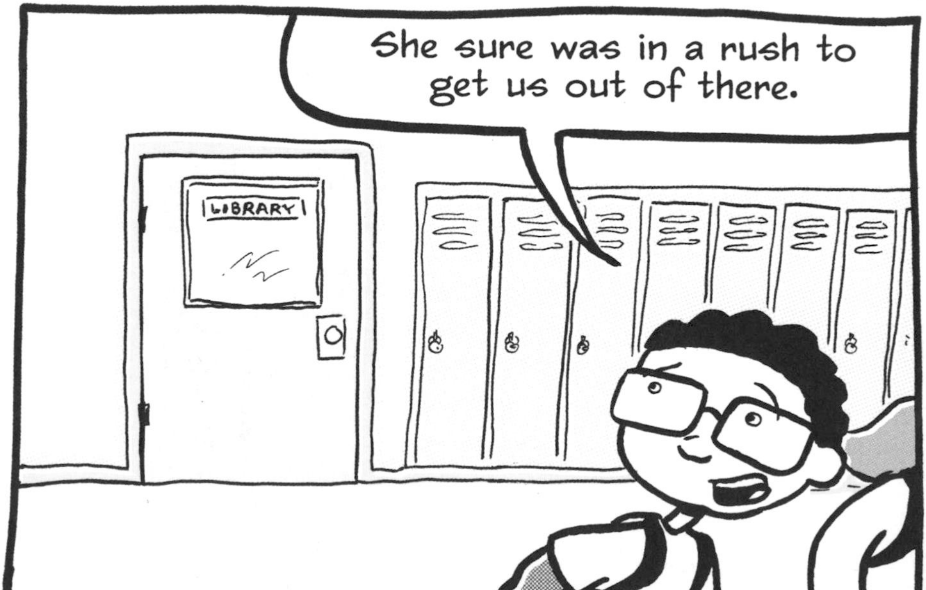
She sure was in a rush to get us out of there.
LIBRARY

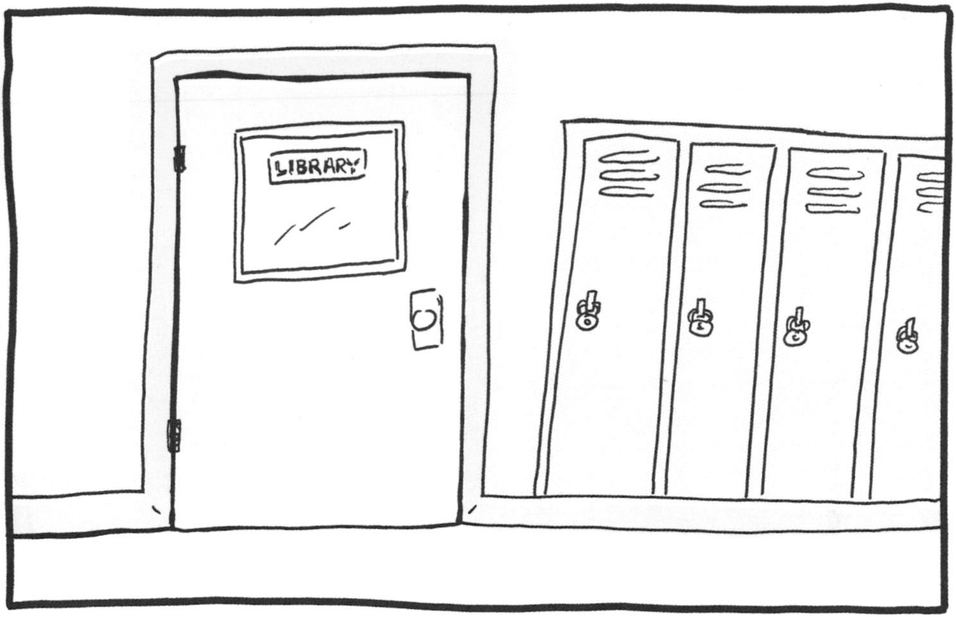
LIBRARY

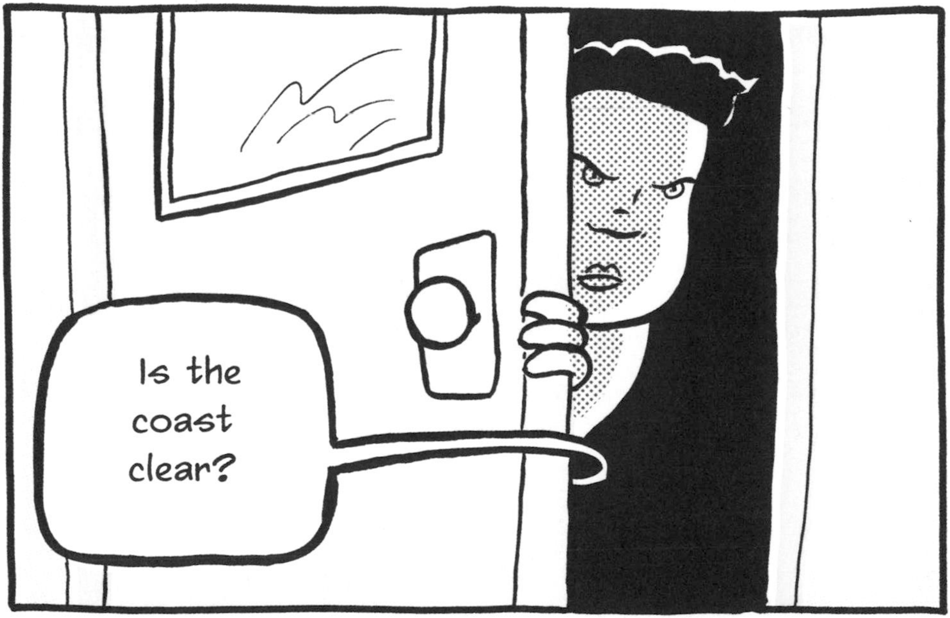
Is the coast clear?

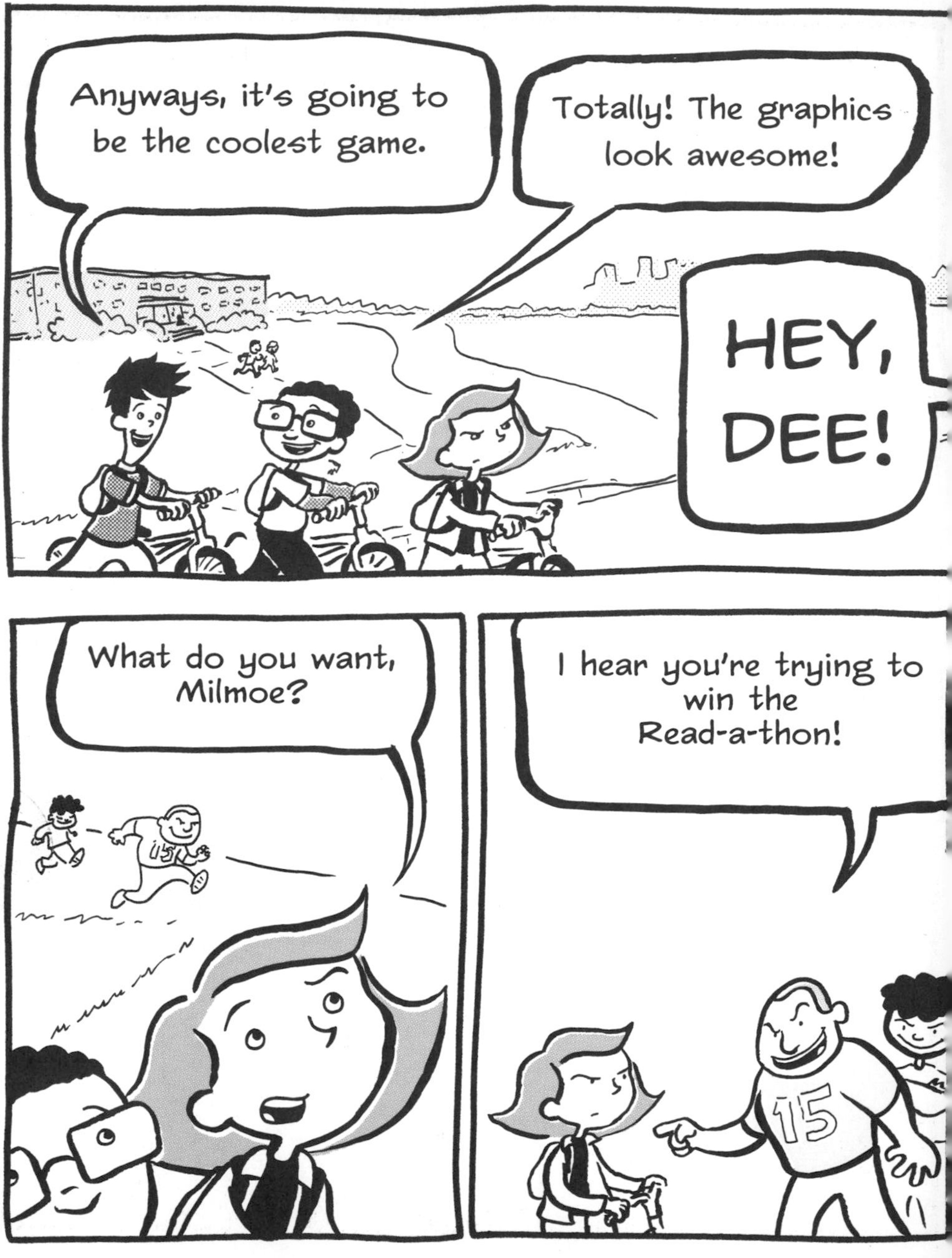
Anyways, it's going to be the coolest game.
Totally! The graphics look awesome!
HEY, DEE!
What do you want, Milmoe?
I hear you're trying to win the Read-a-thon!
15

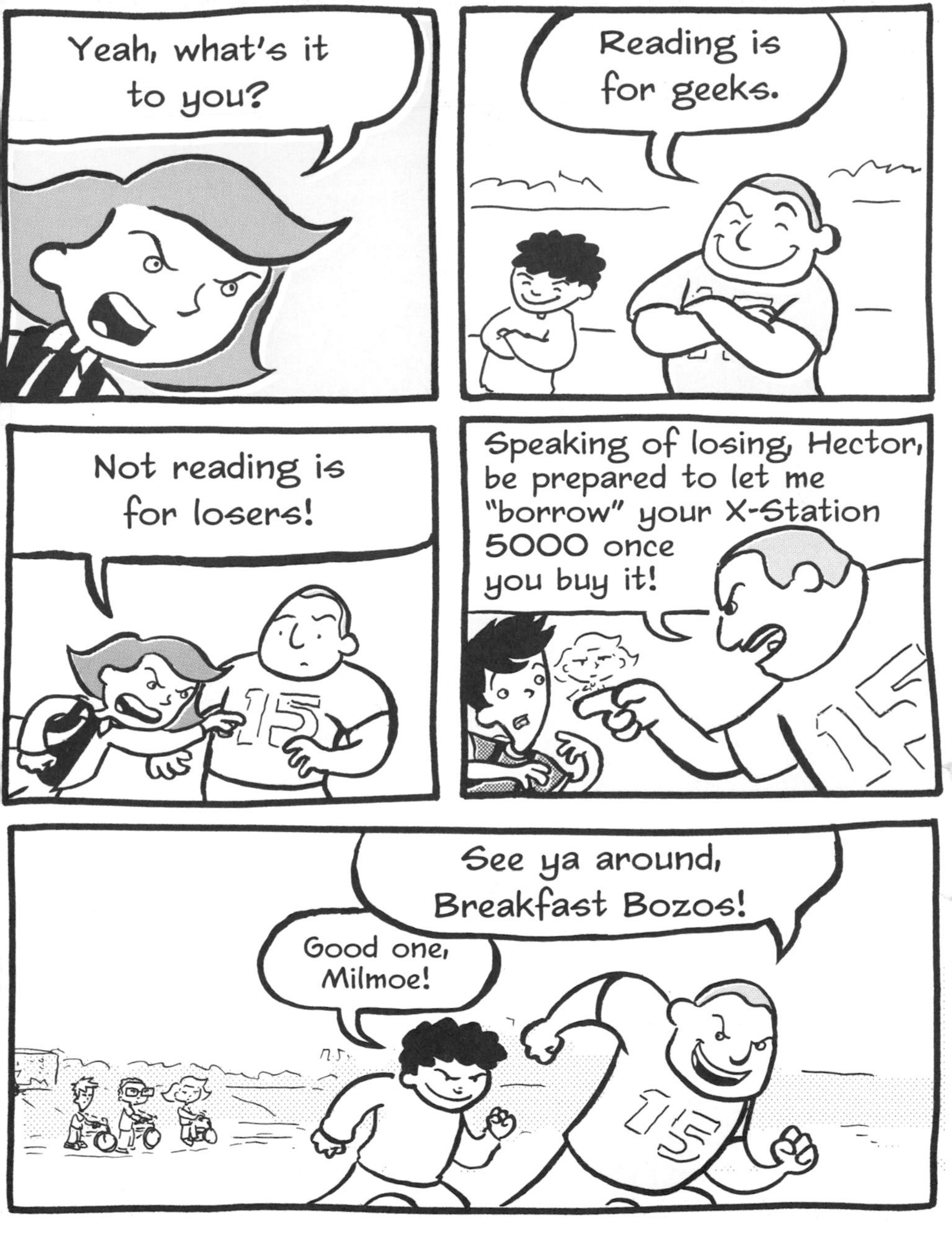

Yeah, what's it to you?
Reading is for geeks.
Not reading is for losers!
Speaking of losing, Hector, be prepared to let me "borrow" your X-Station 5000 once you buy it!
See ya around, Breakfast Bozos!
Good one, Milmoe!

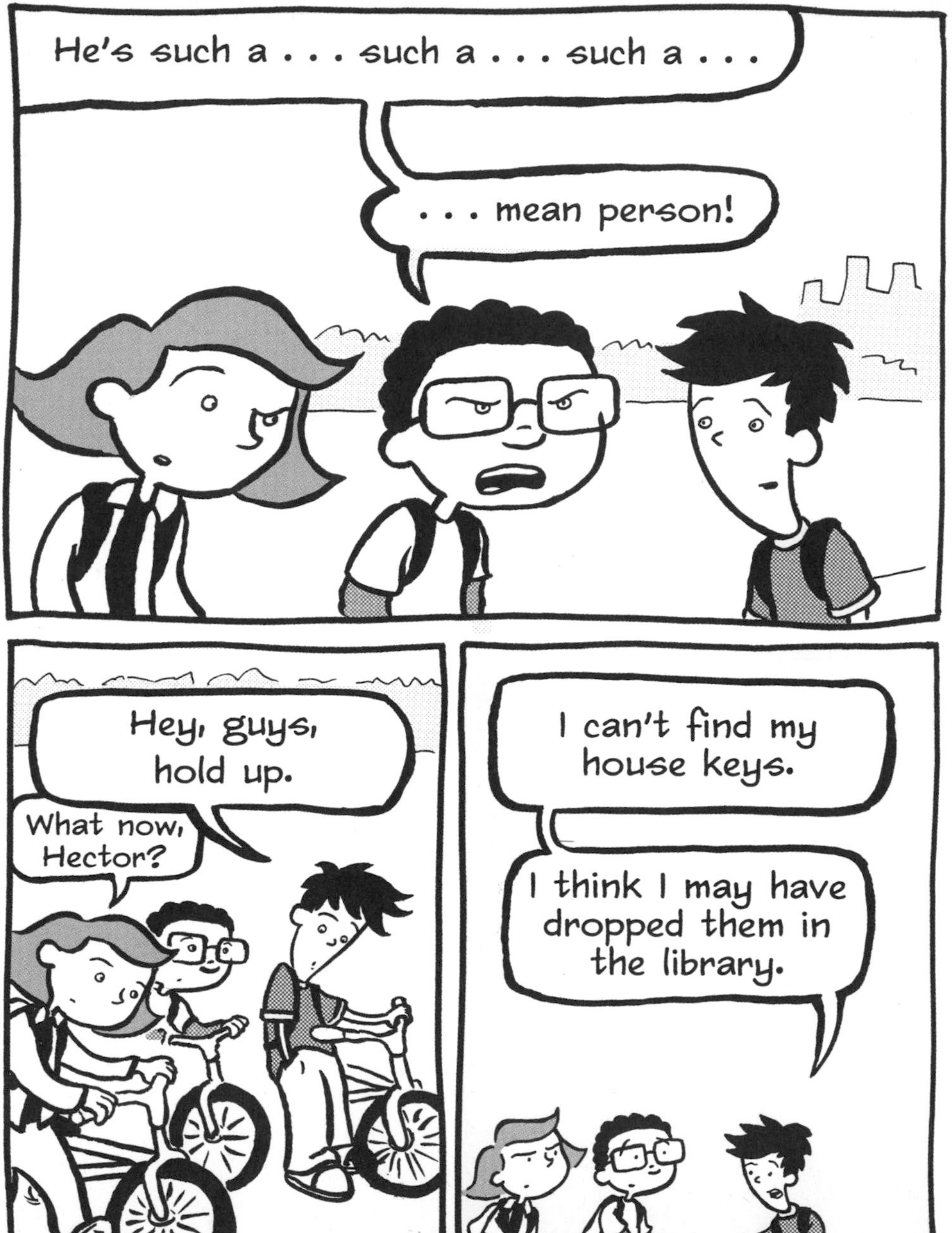
He's such a . . . such a . . . such a . . .
. . . mean person!
Hey, guys, hold up.
What now, Hector?
I can't find my house keys.
I think I may have dropped them in the library.

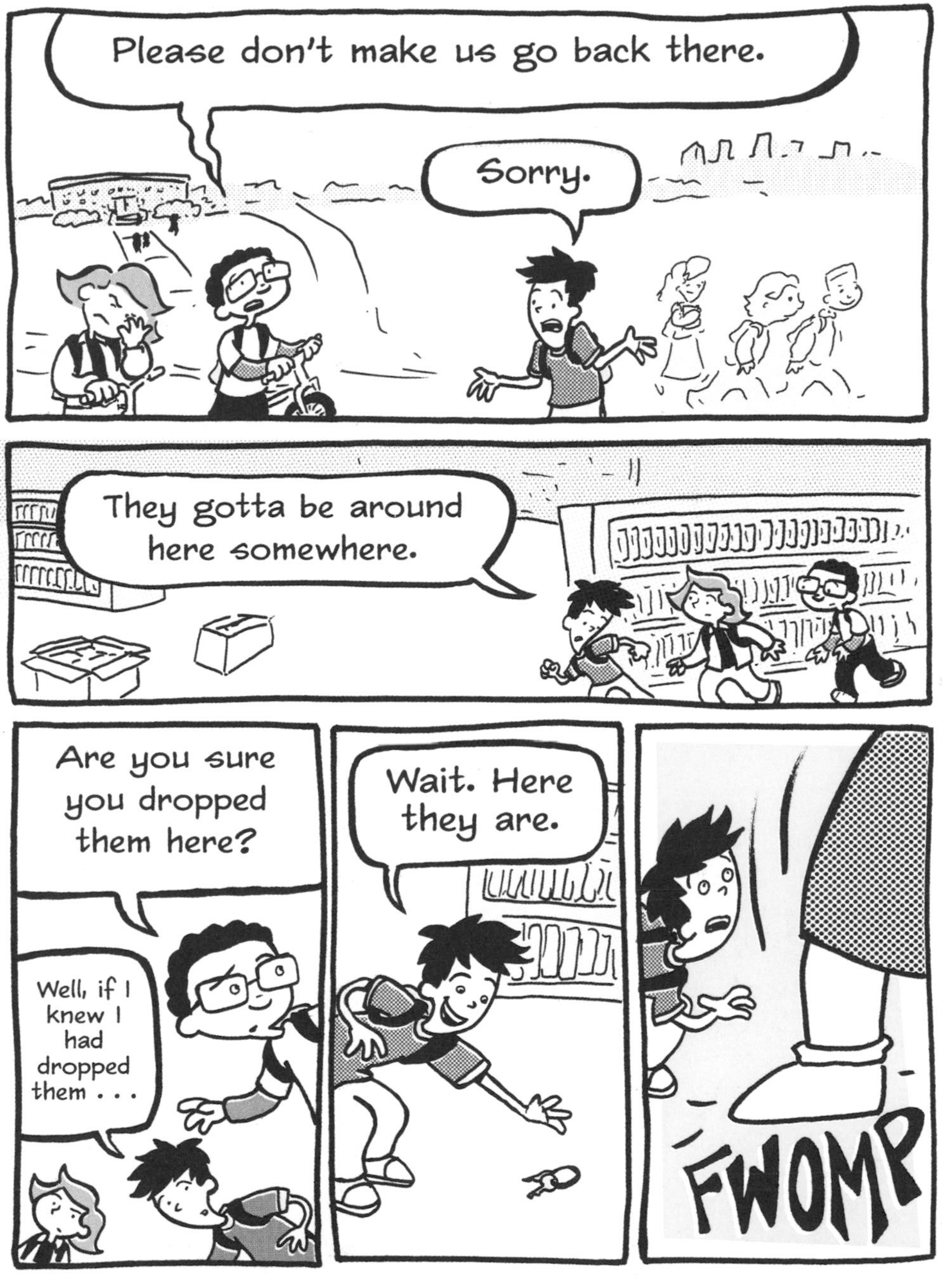
Please don't make us go back there.
Sorry.
They gotta be around here somewhere.
Are you sure you dropped them here?
Well, if I knew I had dropped them . . .
Wait. Here they are.
FWOMP

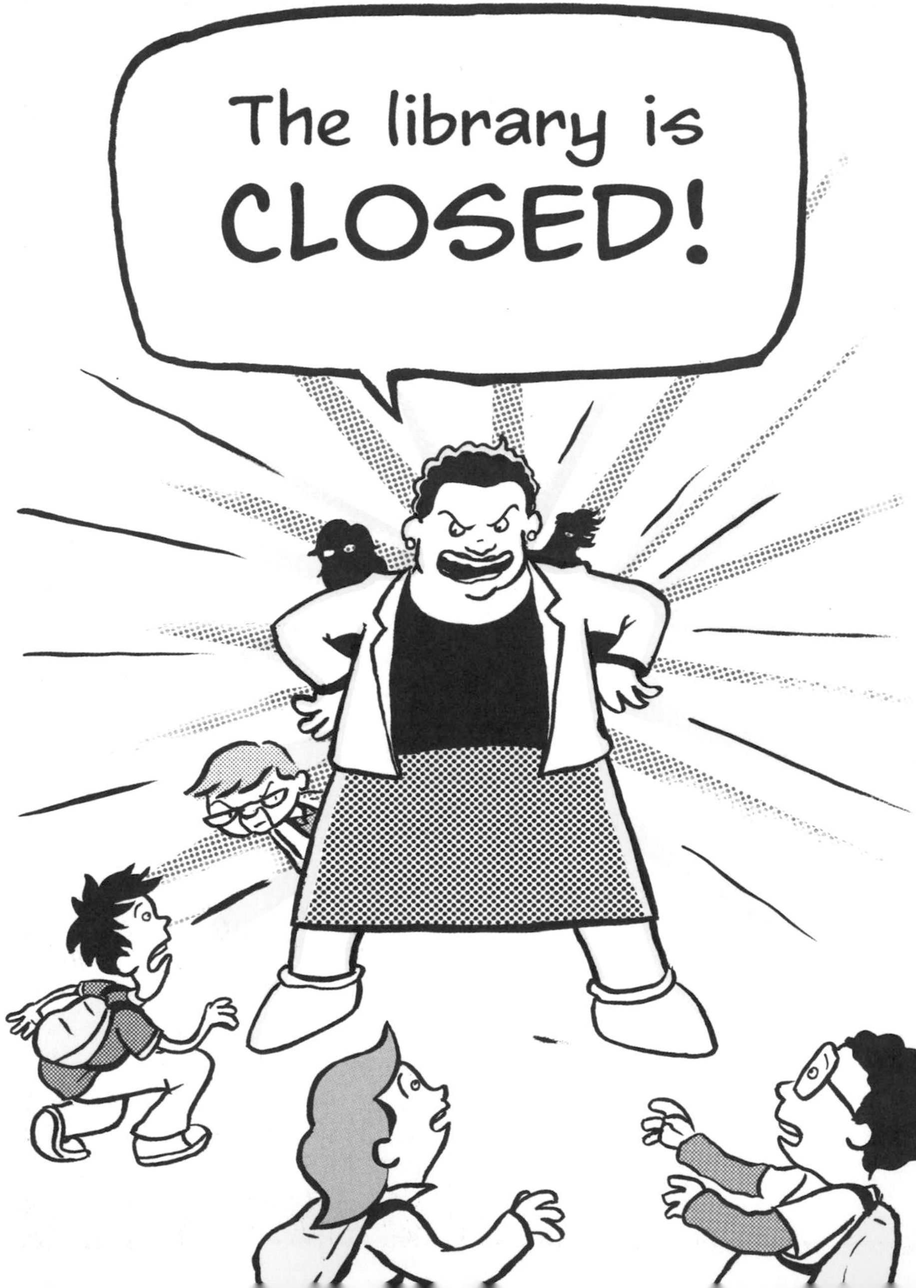
The library is CLOSED!

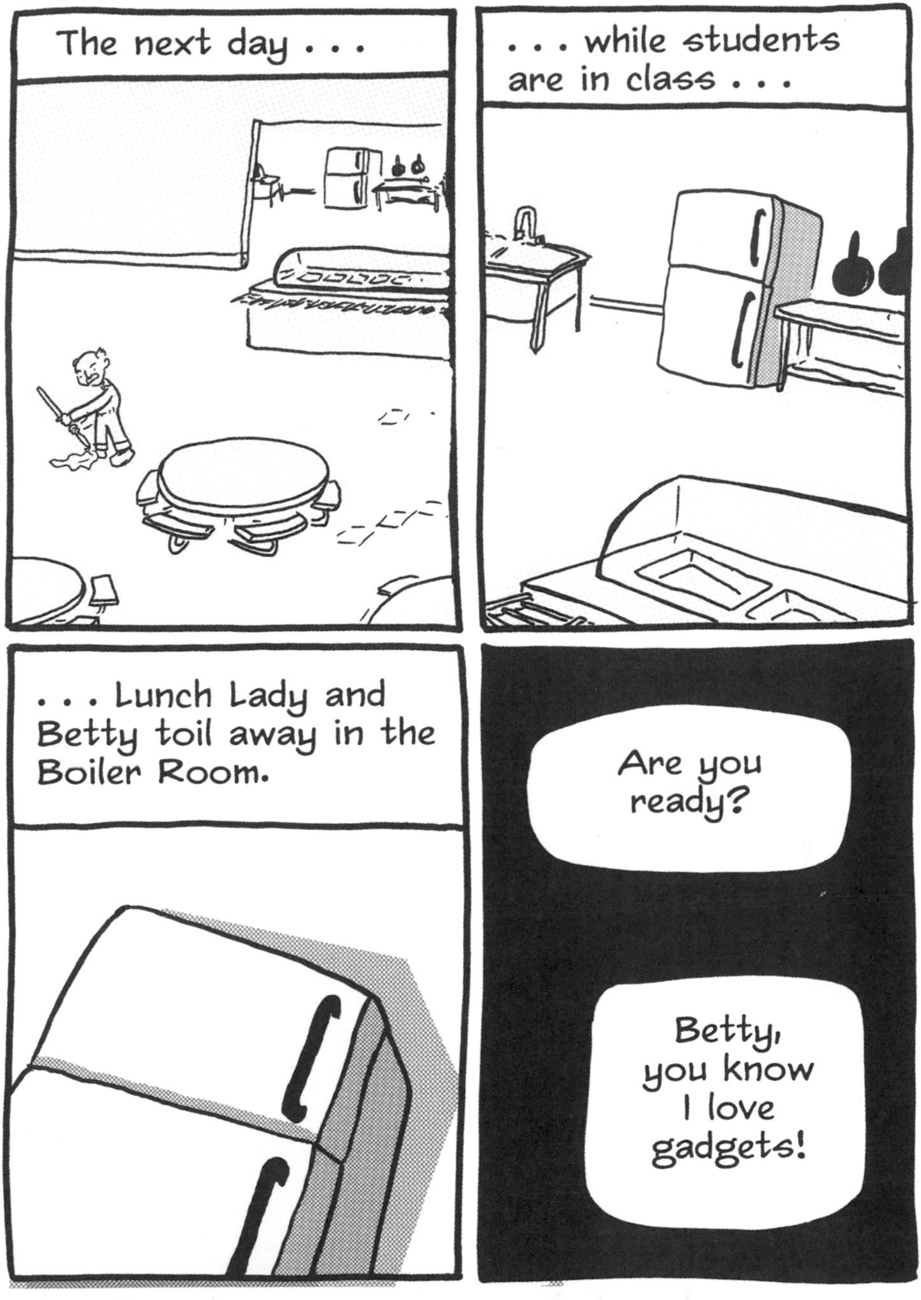
The next day . . .
. . . while students are in class . . .
. . . Lunch Lady and Betty toil away in the Boiler Room.
Are you ready?
Betty, you know I love gadgets!

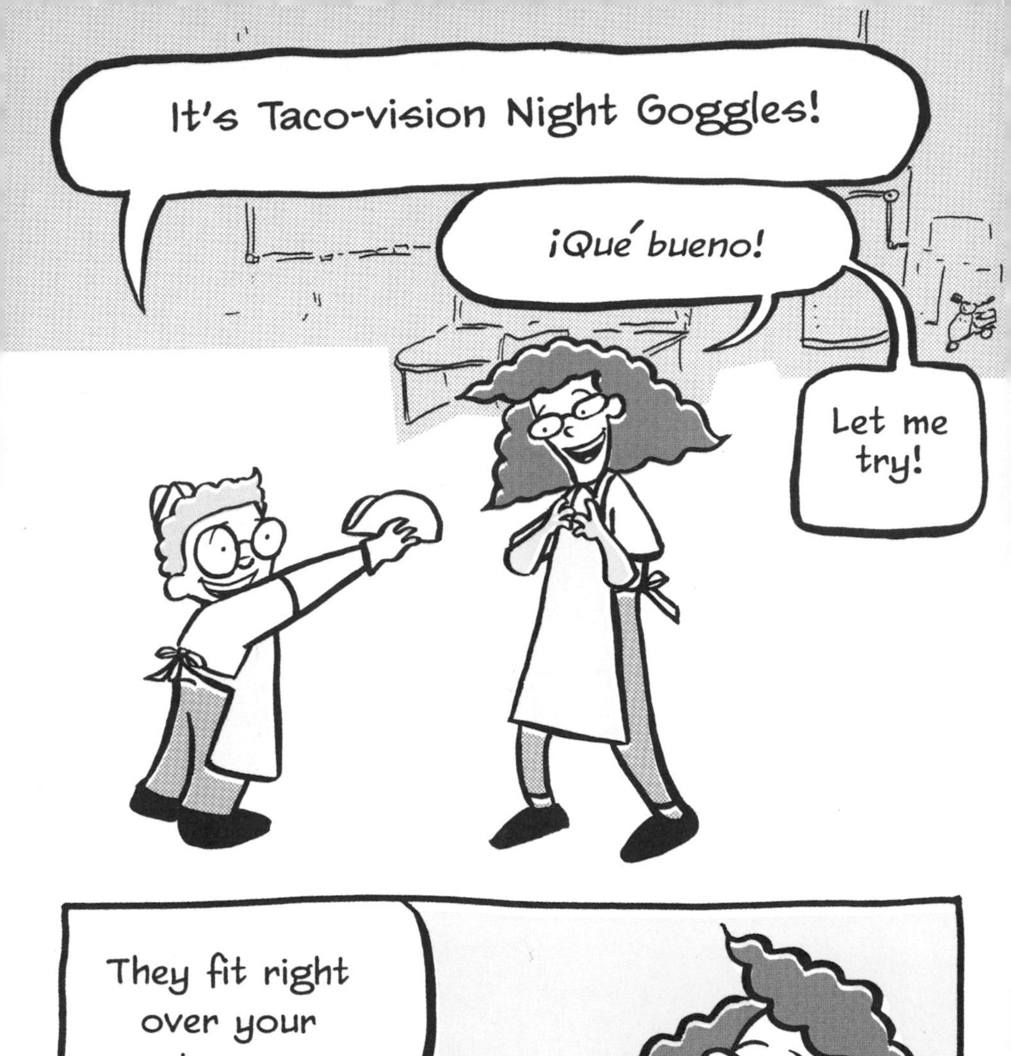
It's Taco-vision Night Goggles!
¡Qué bueno!
Let me try!

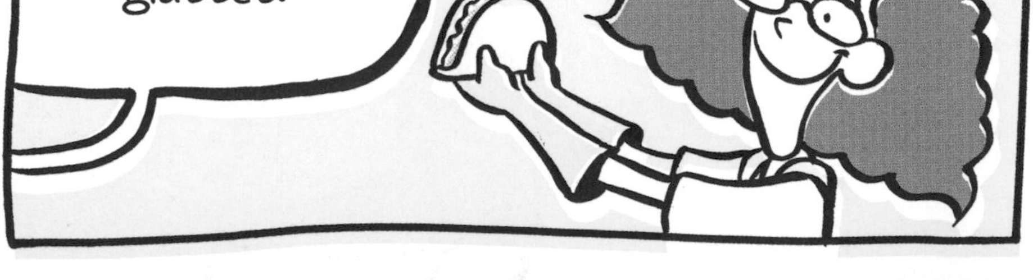
They fit right over your glasses.

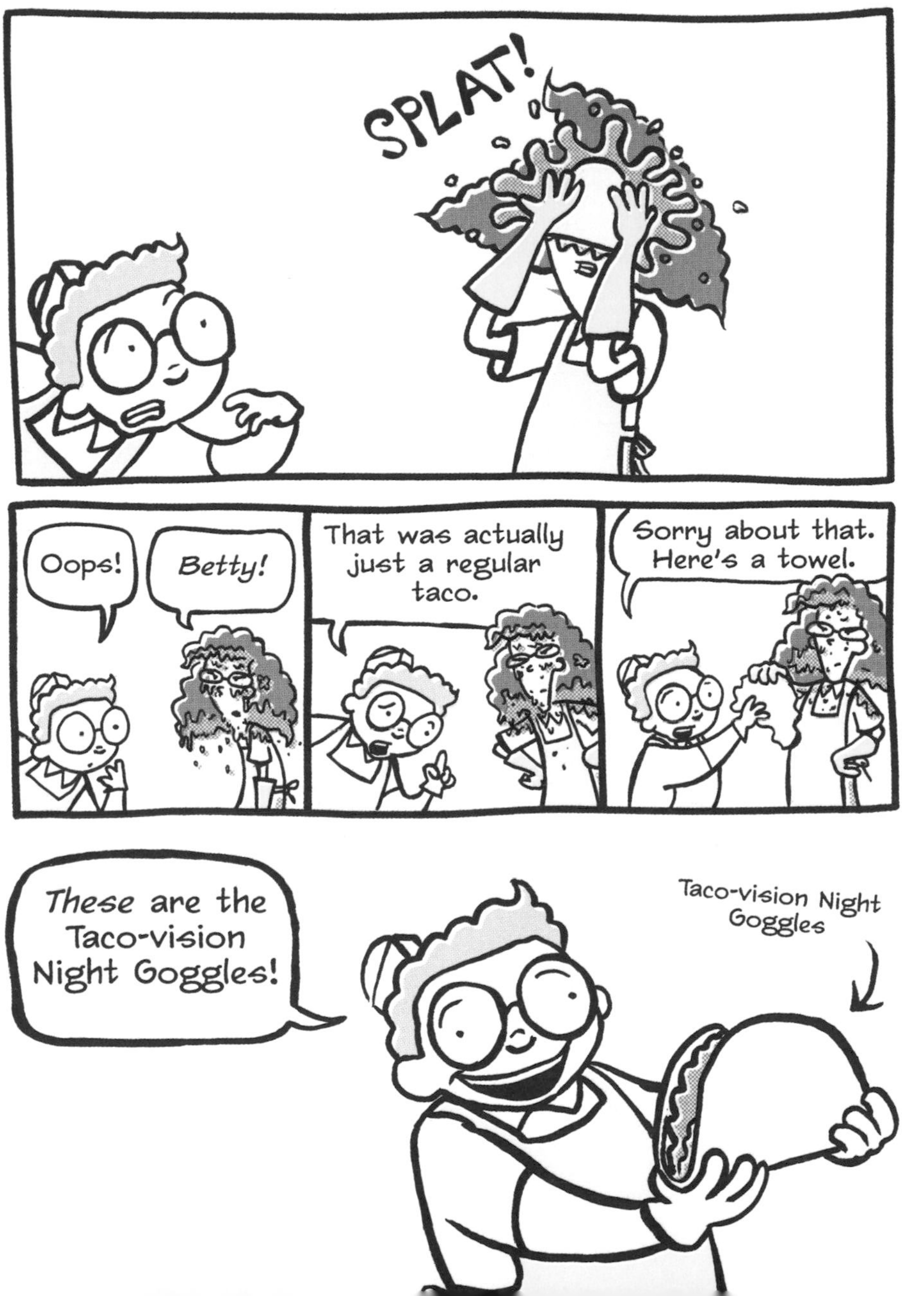
SPLAT!
Oops!
Betty!
That was actually just a regular taco.
Sorry about that. Here's a towel.
These are the Taco-vision Night Goggles!
Taco-vision Night Goggles

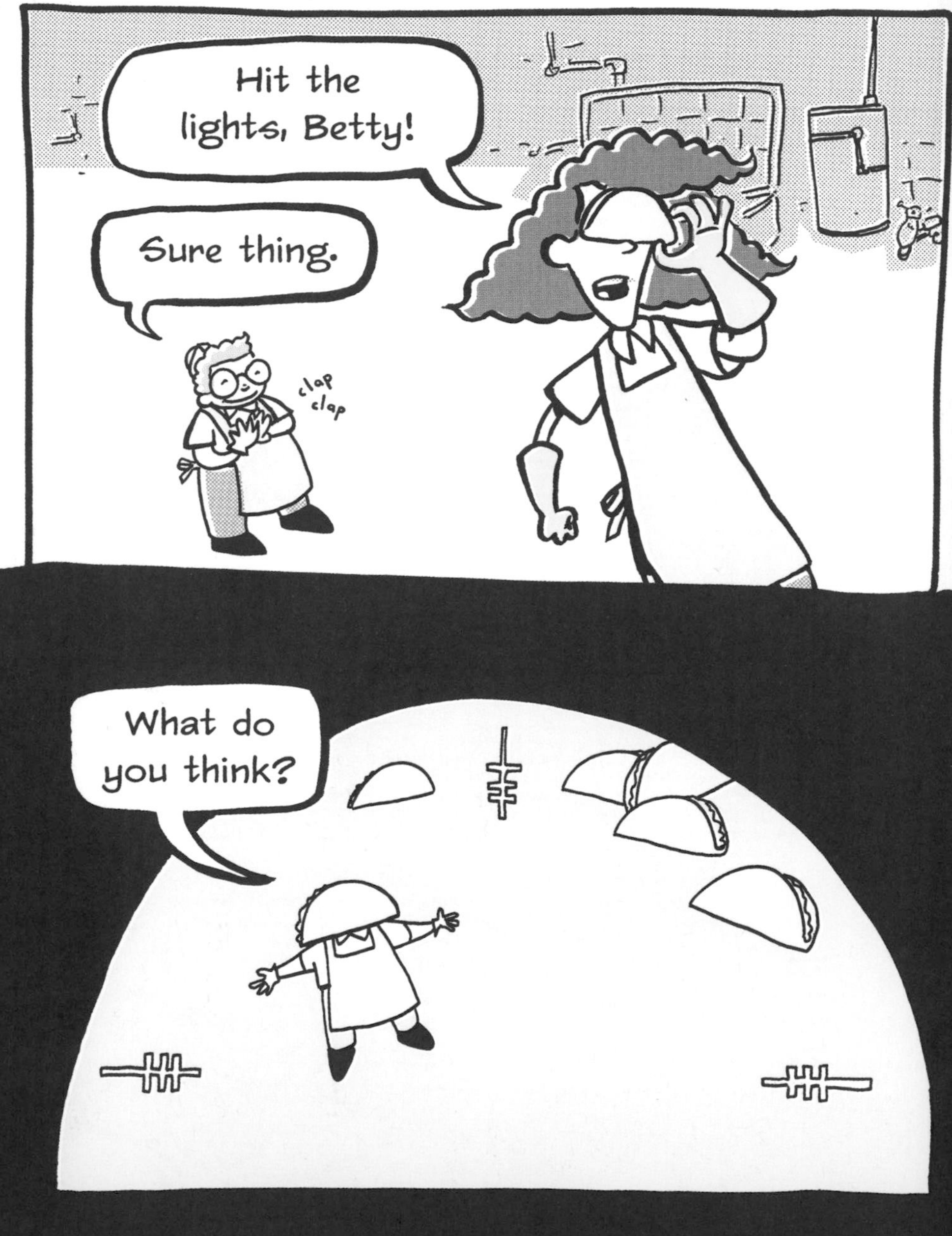
Hit the lights, Betty!
Sure thing.
clap clap
What do you think?

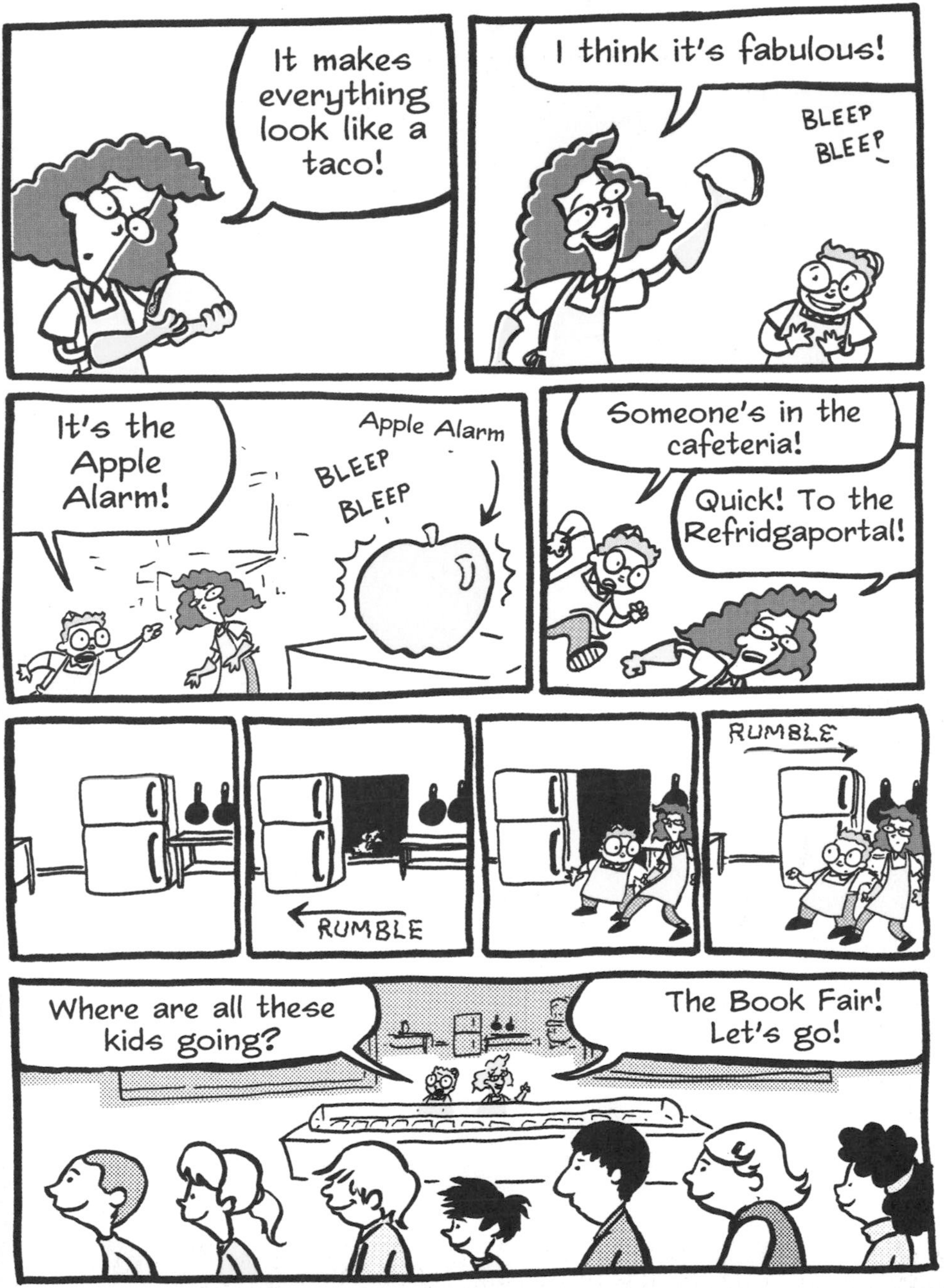

It makes everything look like a taco!
I think it's fabulous!
BLEEP BLEEP
It's the Apple Alarm!
Apple Alarm
BLEEP BLEEP
Someone's in the cafeteria!
Quick! To the Refridgaportal!
RUMBLE
RUMBLE
Where are all these kids going?
The Book Fair! Let's go!

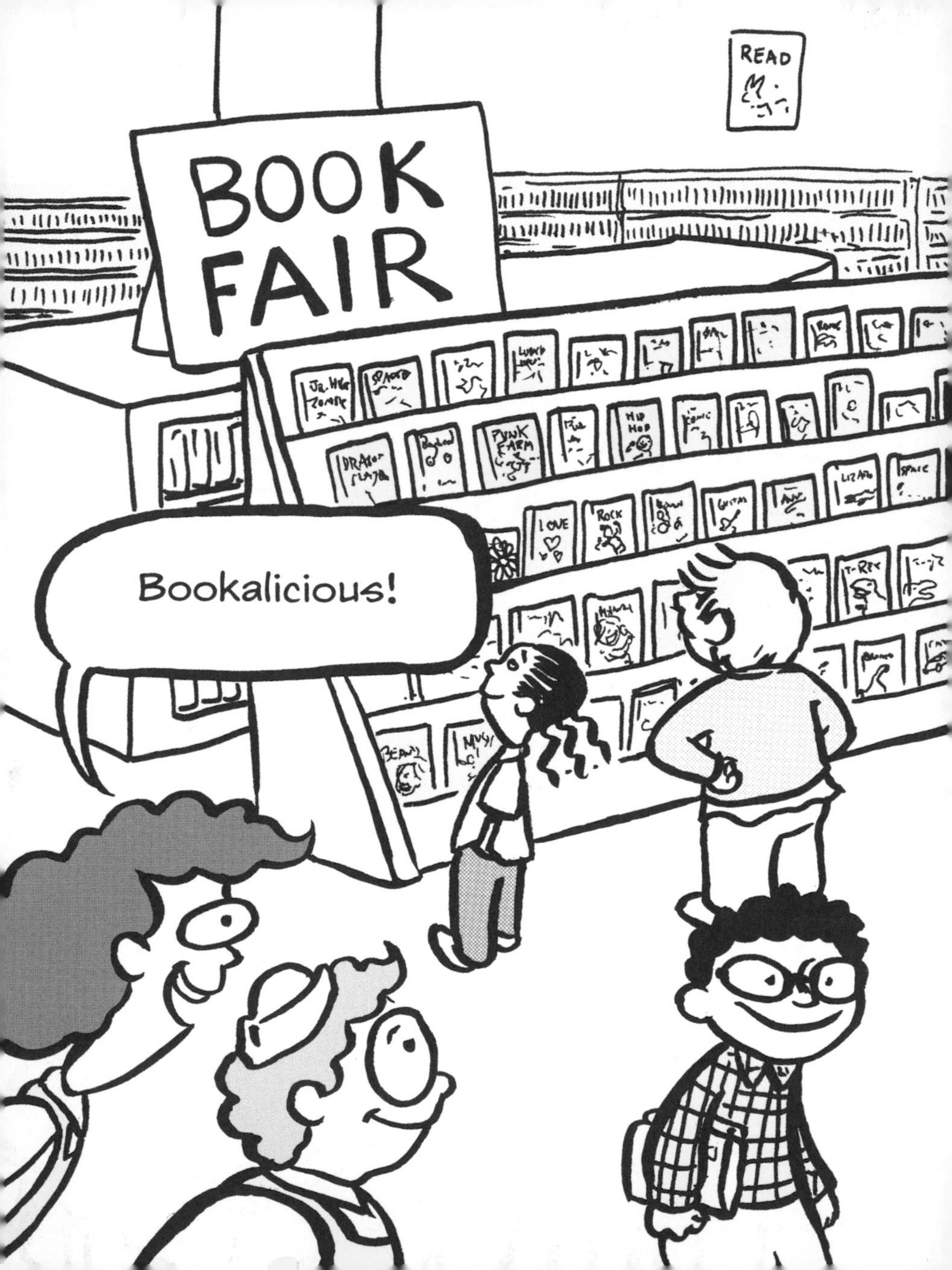
READ
BOOK FAIR
Bookalicious!

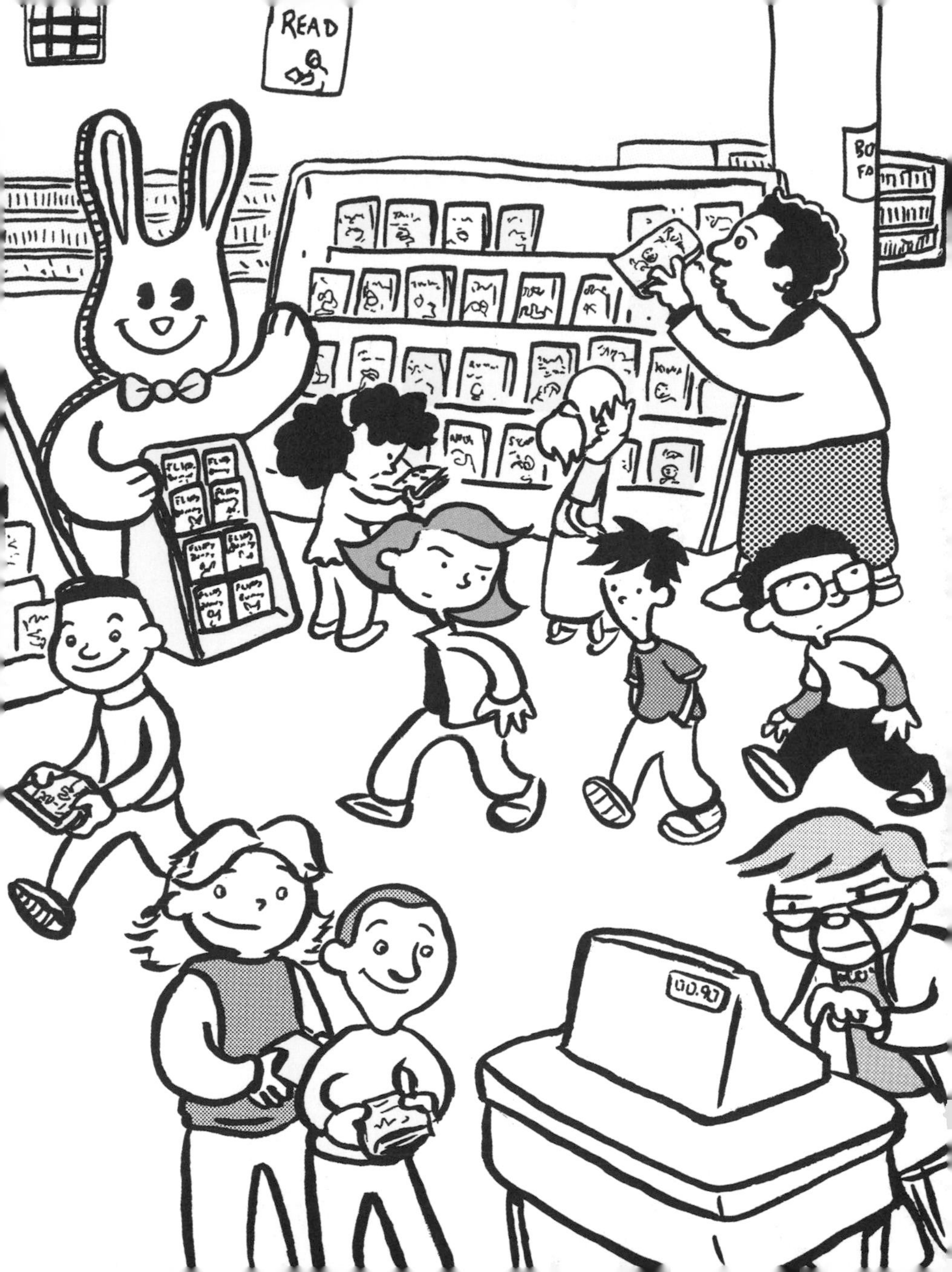
READ

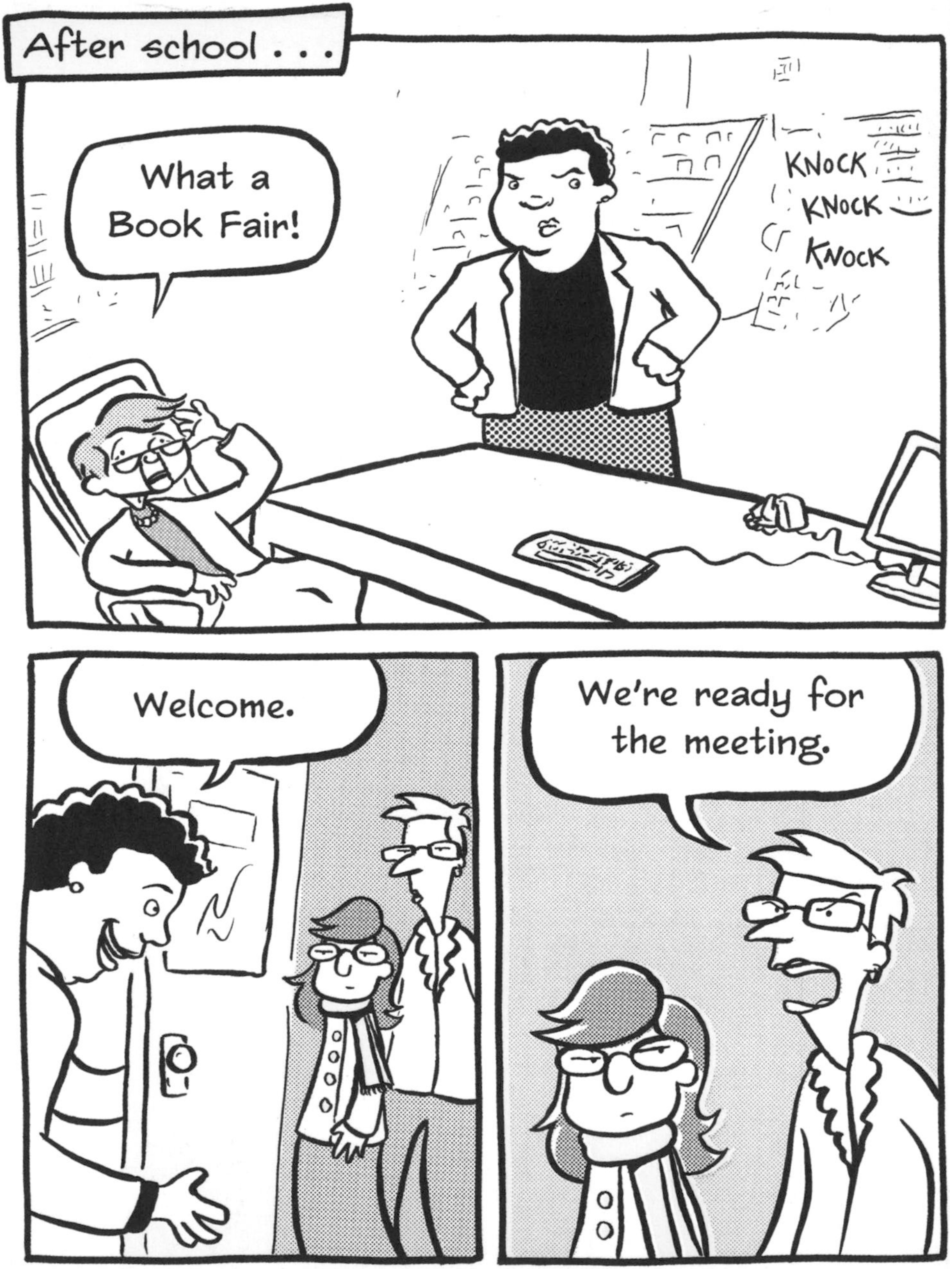
After school . . .
What a Book Fair!
KNOCK KNOCK KNOCK
Welcome.
We're ready for the meeting.

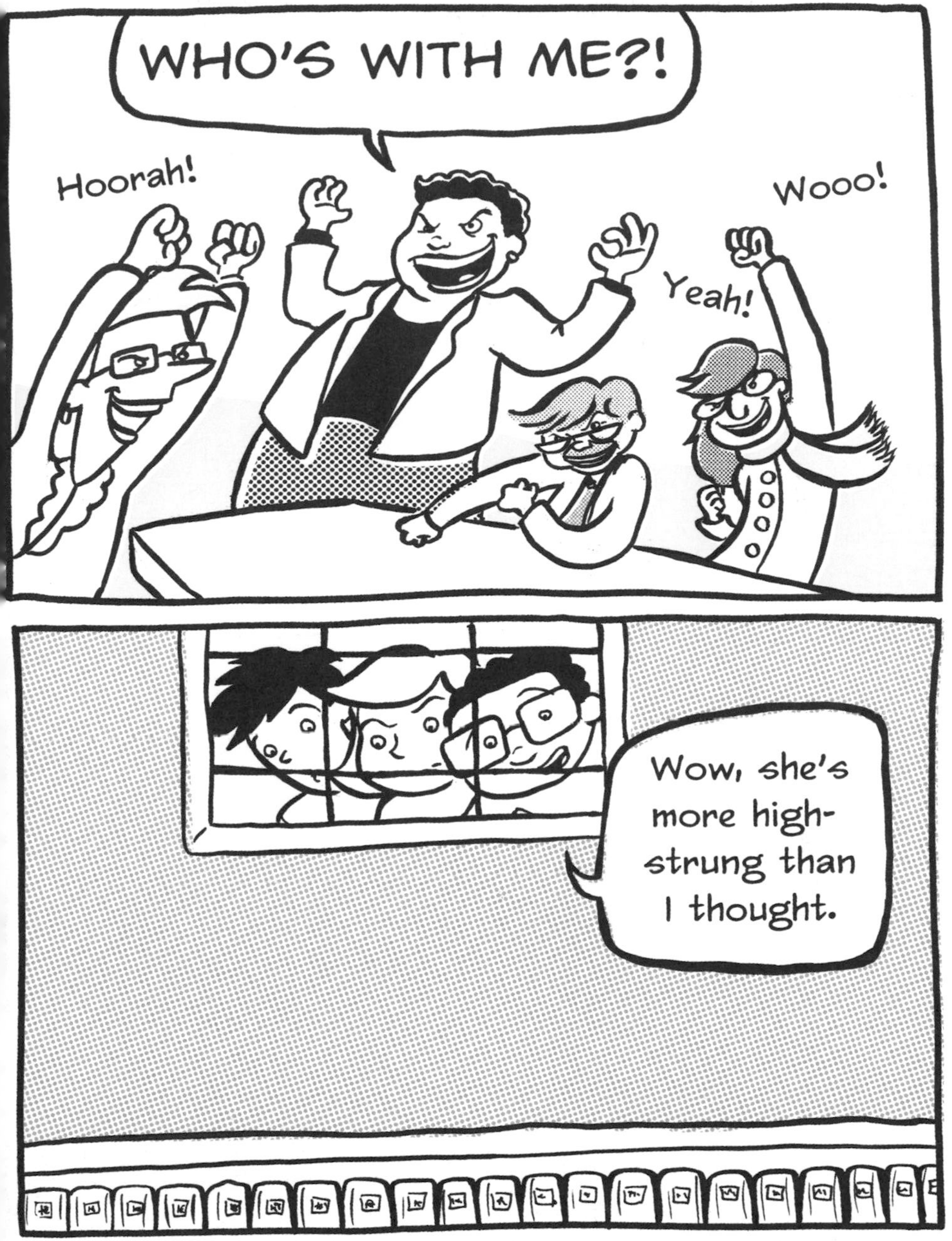
WHO'S WITH ME?!
Hoorah!
Yeah!
Wooo!
Wow, she's more high-strung than I thought.

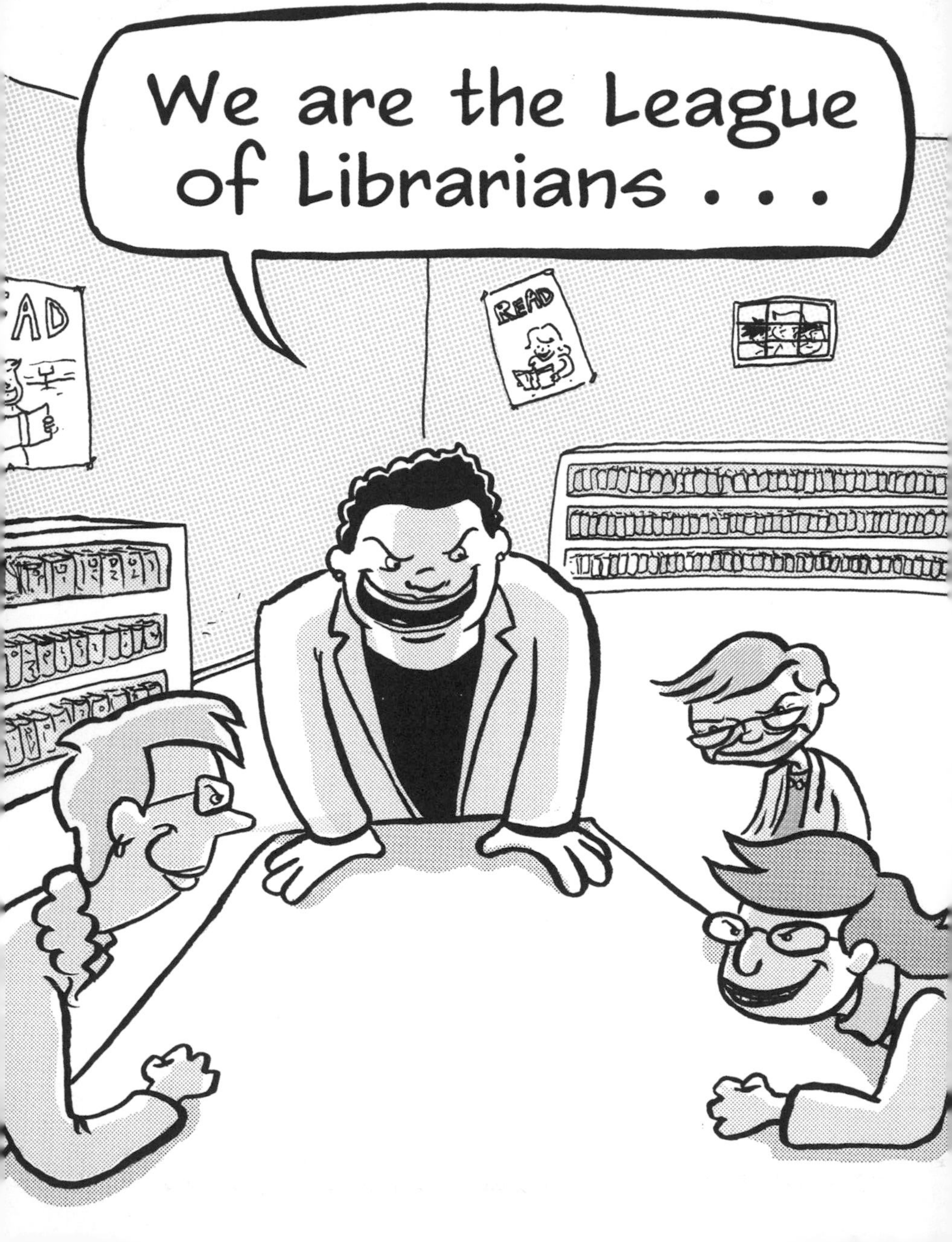
We are the League of Librarians . . .
READ

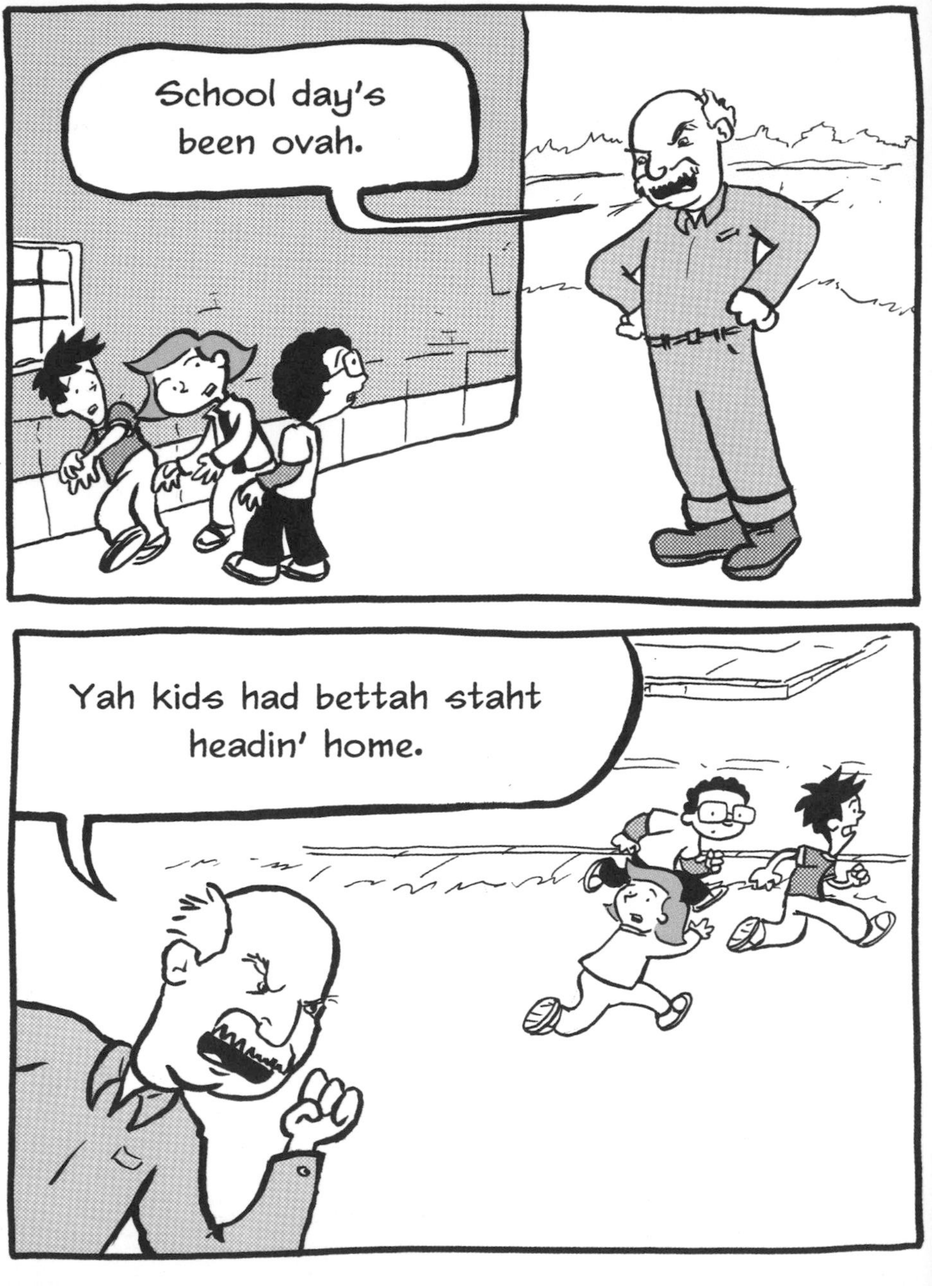
School day's been ovah.
Yah kids had bettah staht headin' home.

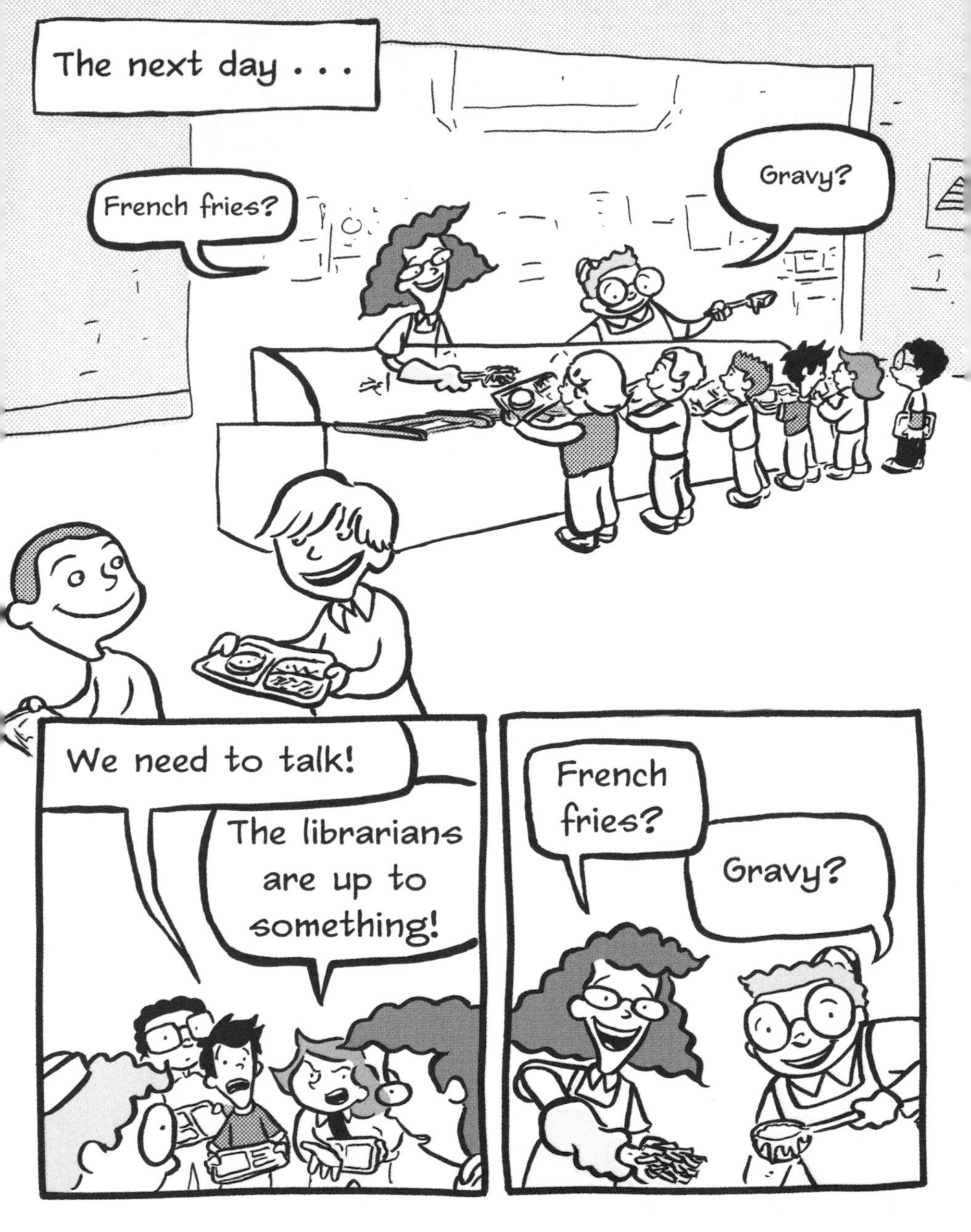

The next day . . .
French fries?
Gravy?
We need to talk!
The librarians are up to something!
French fries?
Gravy?

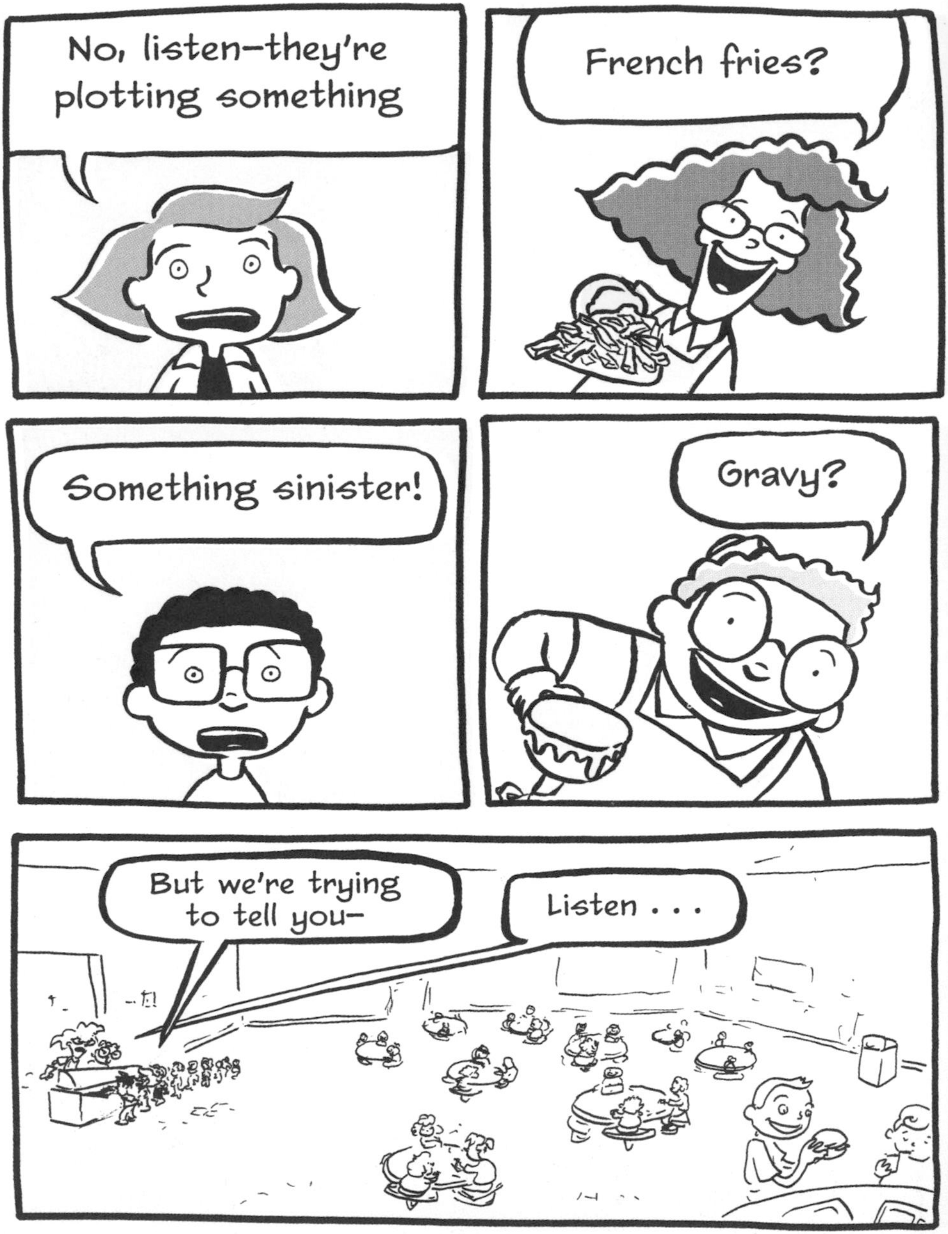
No, listen—they're plotting something
French fries?
Something sinister!
Gravy?
But we're trying to tell you—
Listen . . .

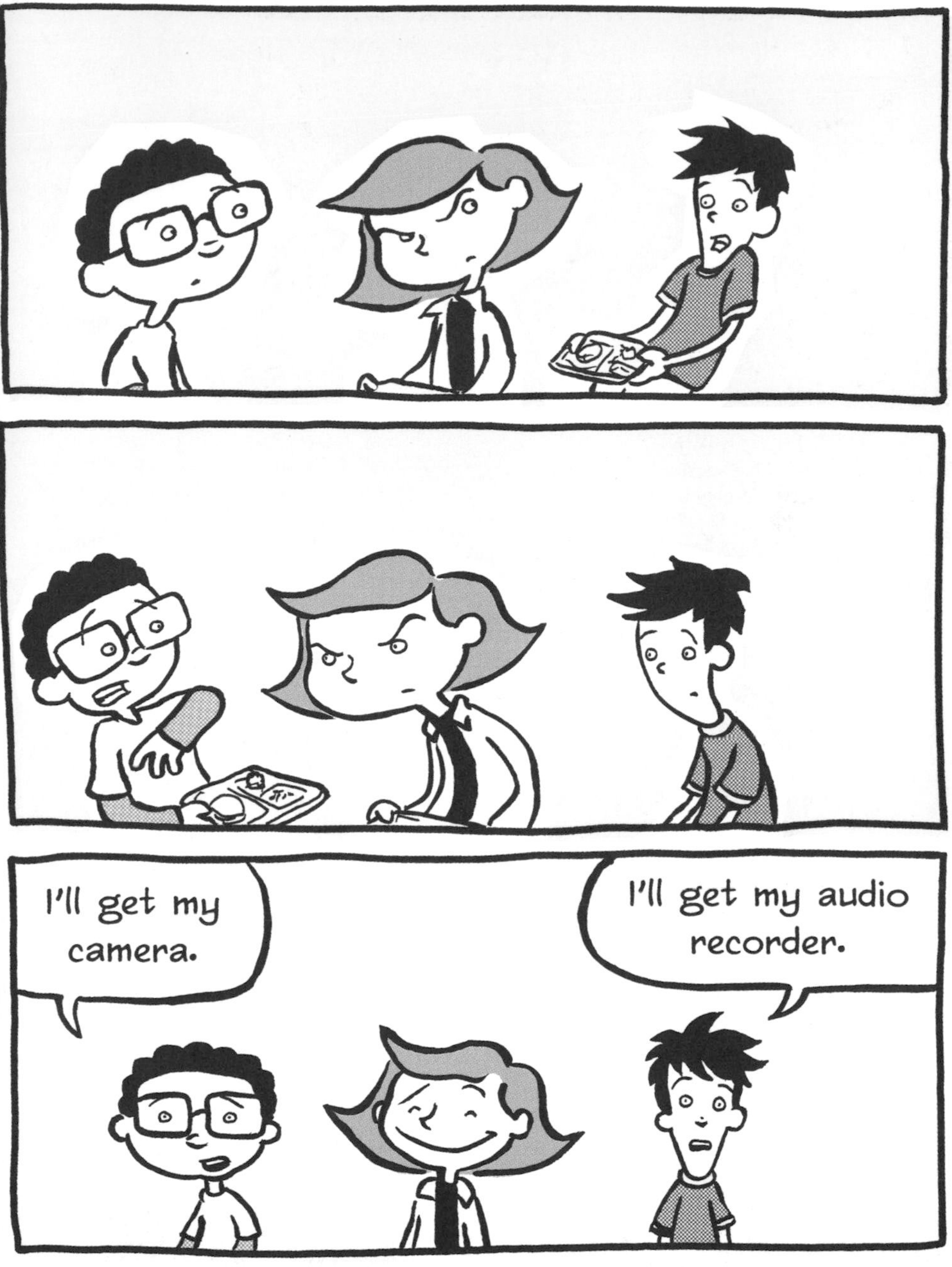
I'll get my camera.
I'll get my audio recorder.

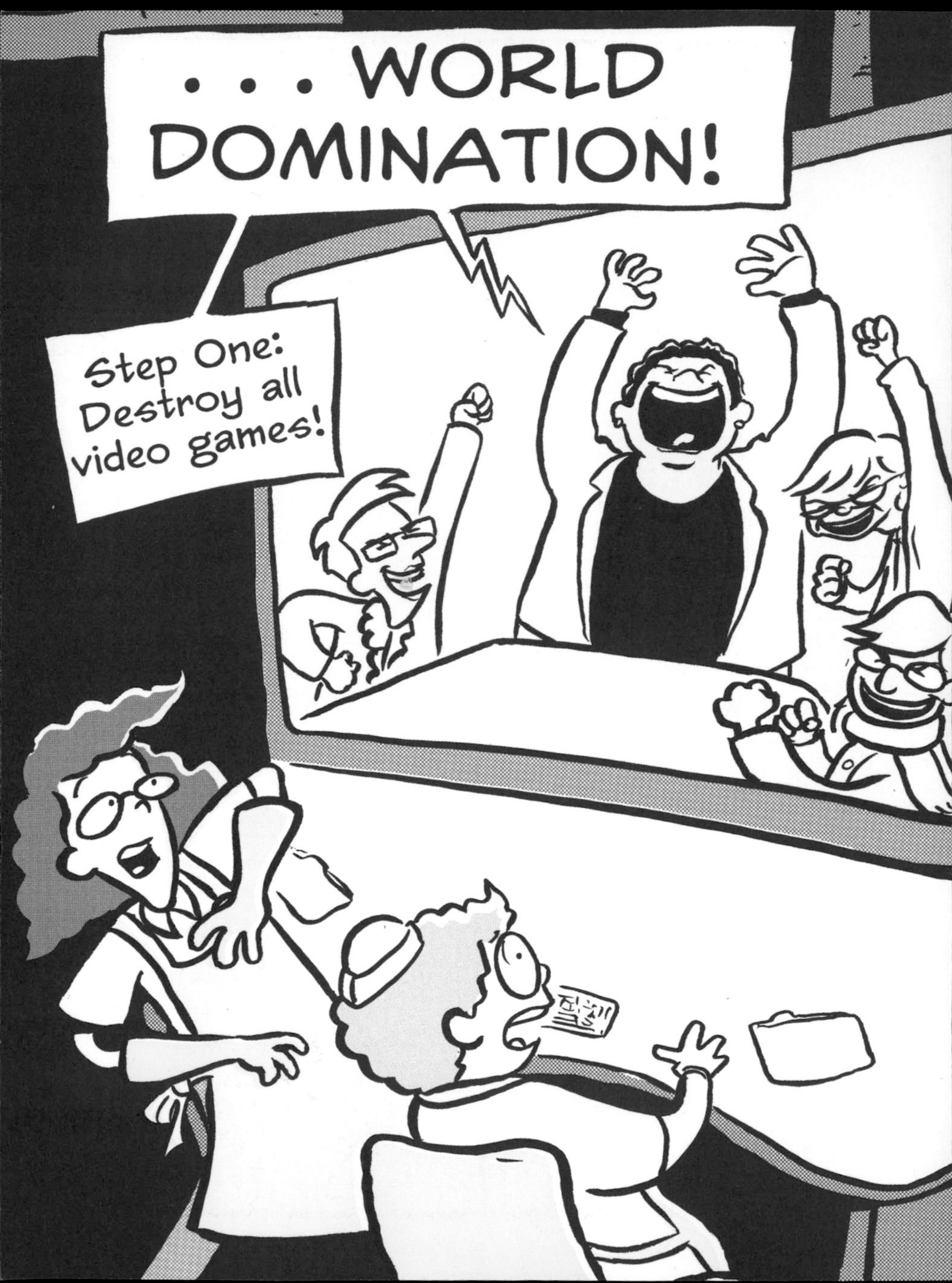
. . . WORLD DOMINATION!
Step One: Destroy all video games!

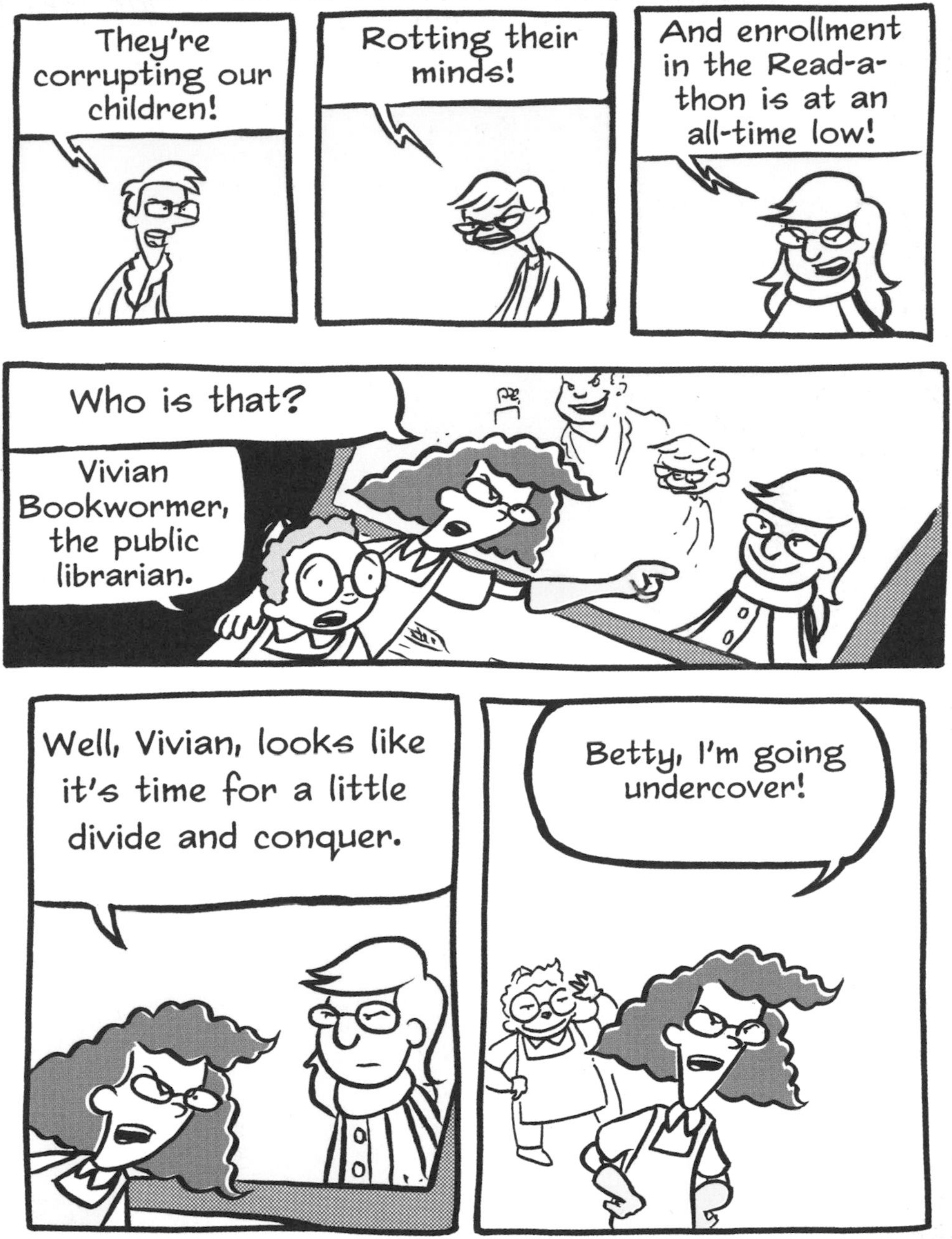
They're corrupting our children!
Rotting their minds!
And enrollment in the Read-a-thon is at an all-time low!
Who is that?
Vivian Bookwormer, the public librarian.
Well, Vivian, looks like it's time for a little divide and conquer.
Betty, I'm going undercover!

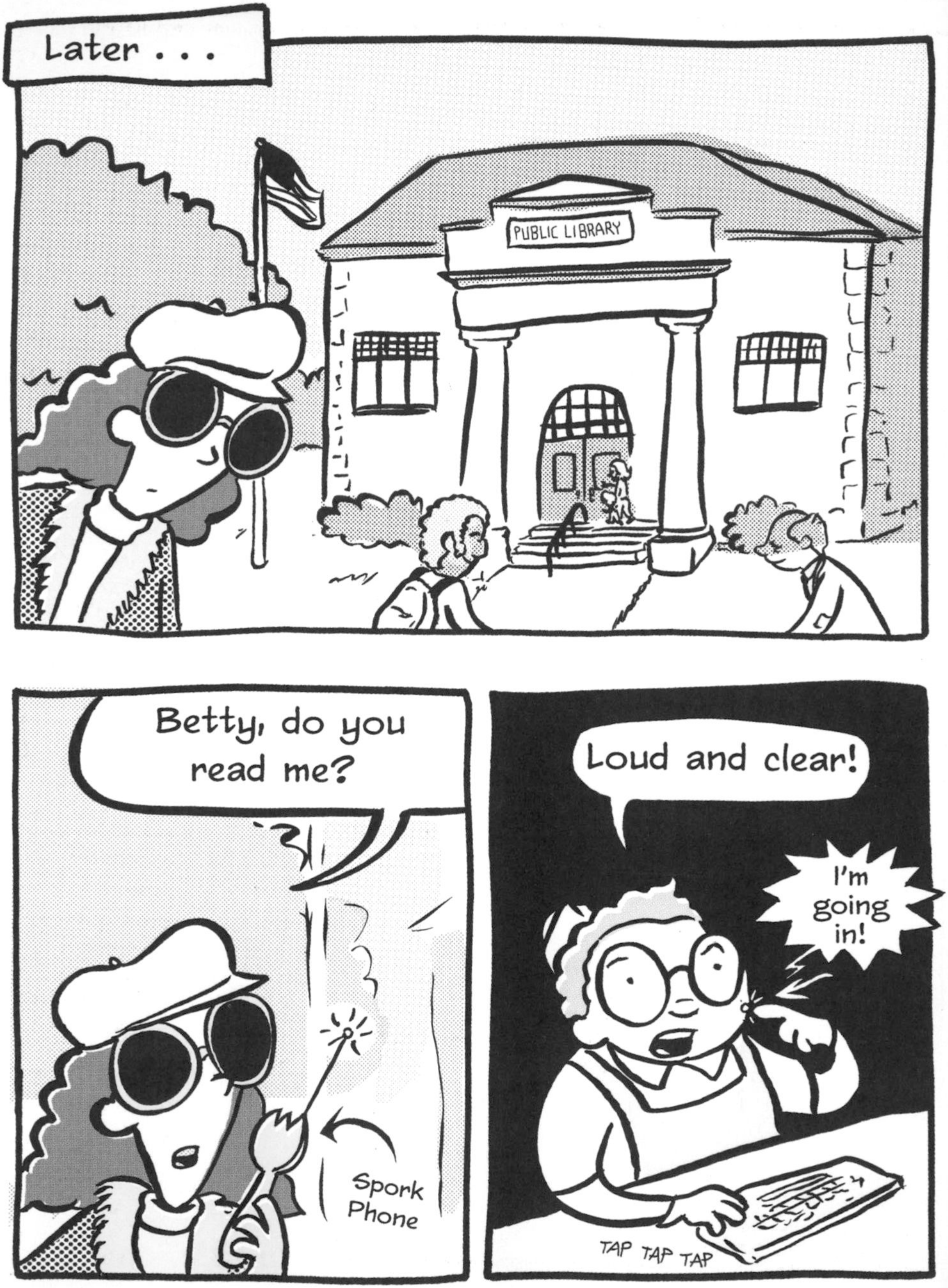
Later . . .
PUBLIC LIBRARY
Betty, do you read me?
Spork Phone
Loud and clear!
I'm going in!
TAP TAP TAP

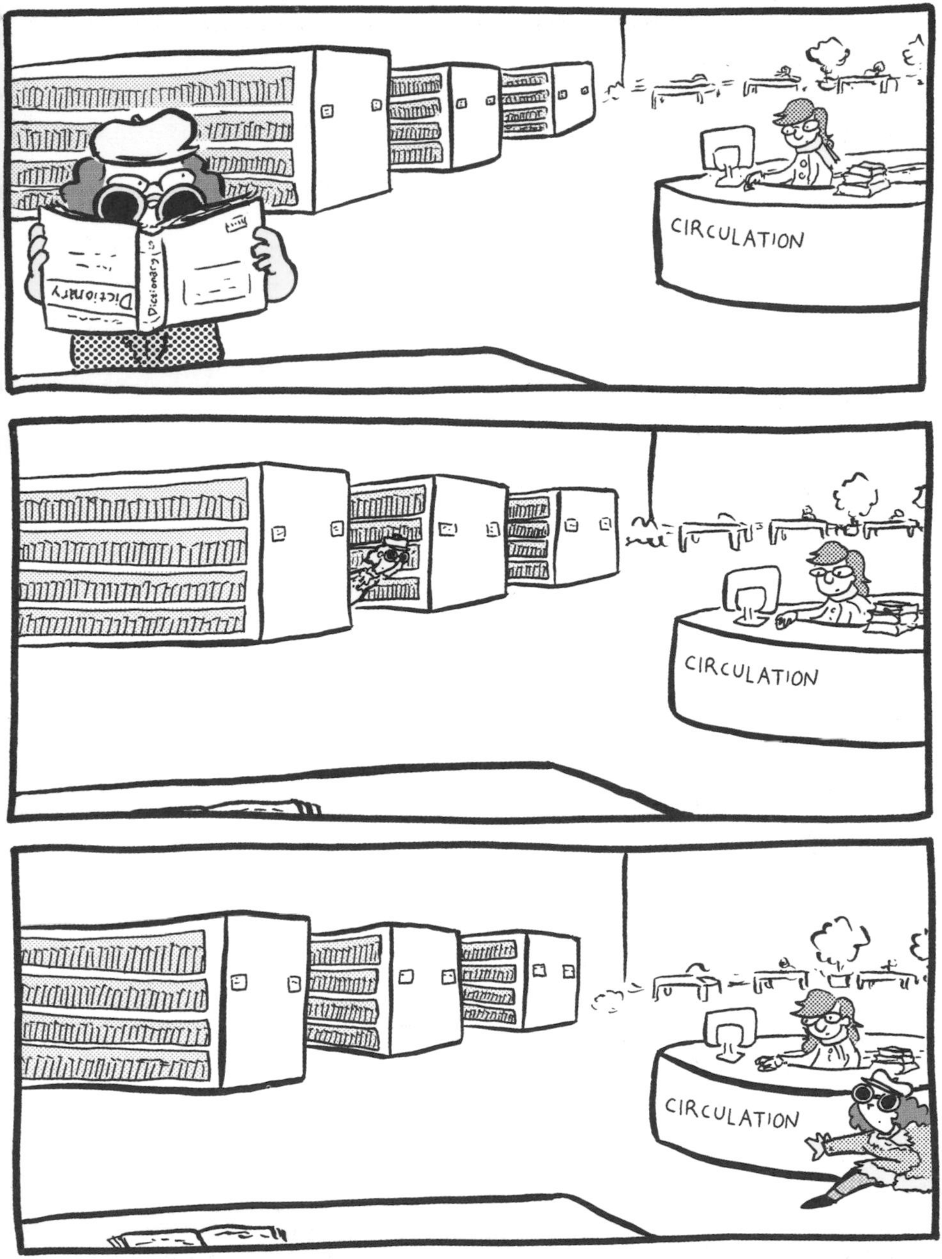
Dictionary
Dictionary
CIRCULATION
CIRCULATION
CIRCULATION

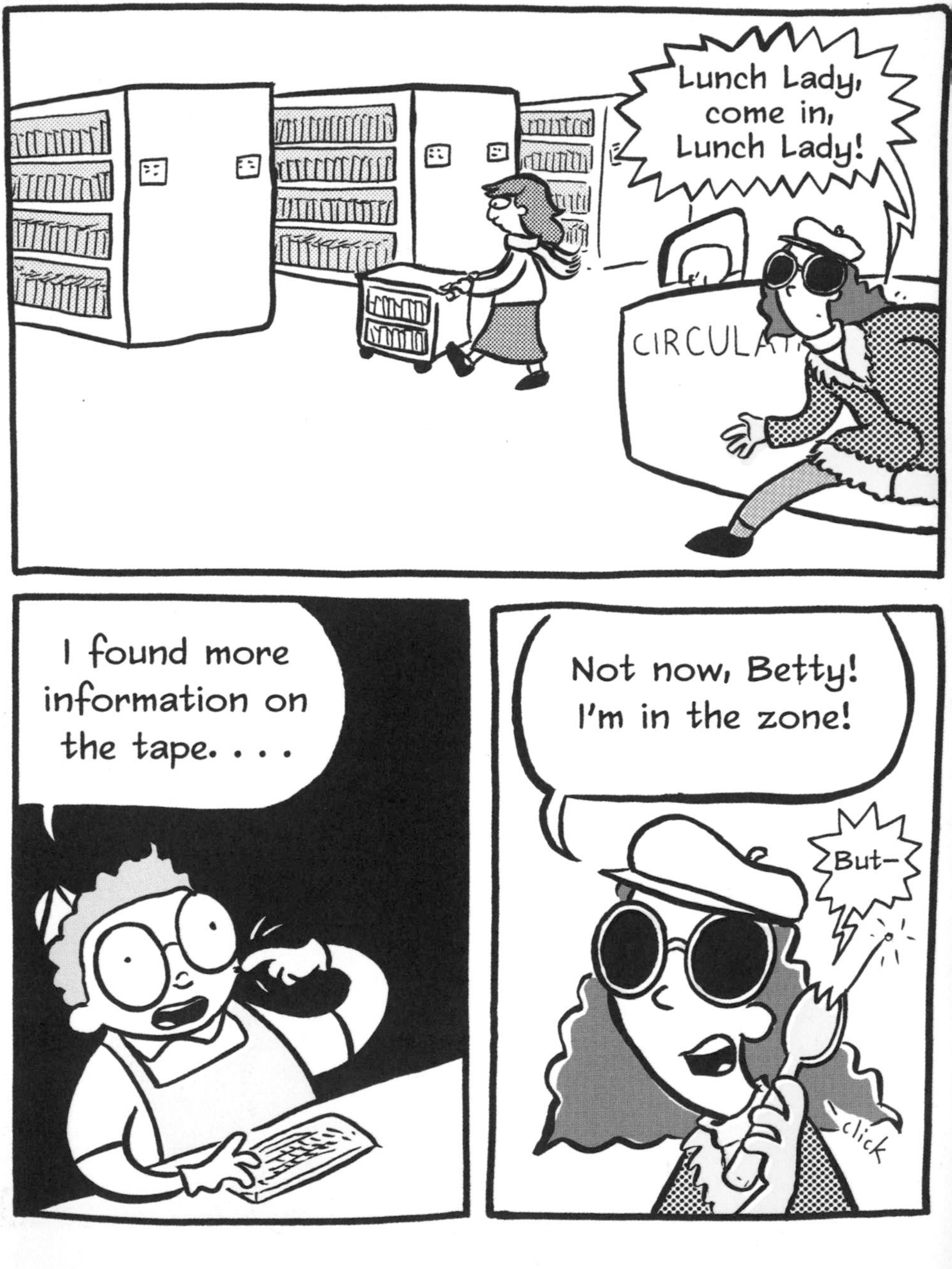
Lunch Lady, come in, Lunch Lady!
CIRCULA
I found more information on the tape. . . .
Not now, Betty! I'm in the zone!
But—
click

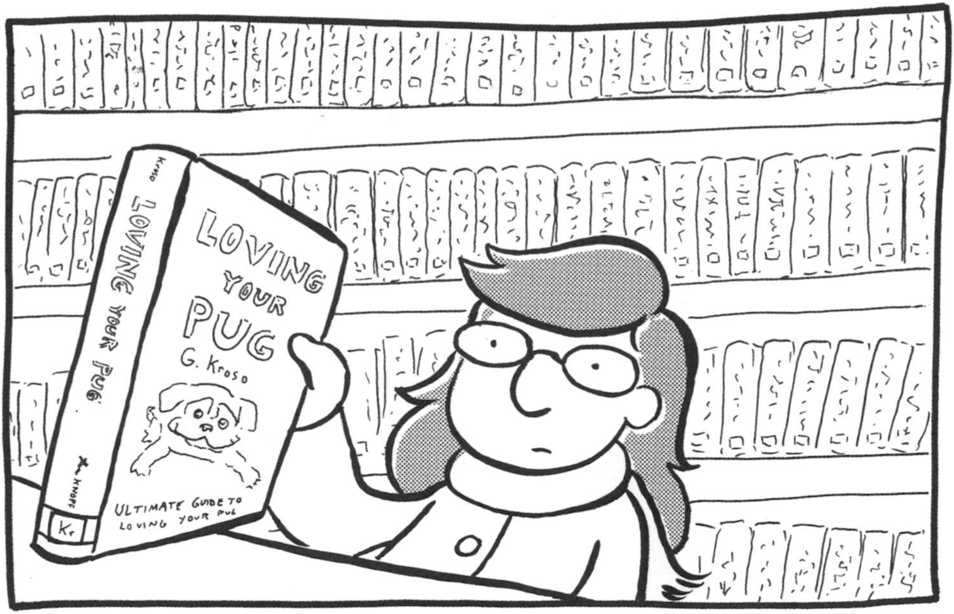
LOVING YOUR PUG
G. Kroso
ULTIMATE GUIDE TO LOVING YOUR PUG
KNOPF
Kr

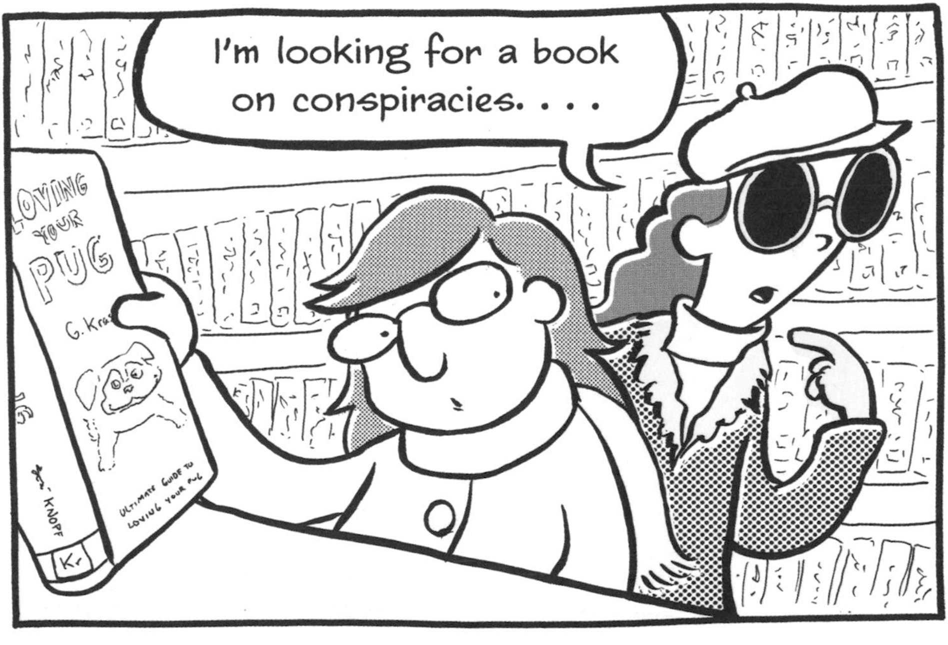
I'm looking for a book on conspiracies. . . .
KNOPF
ULTIMATE GUIDE TO LOVING YOUR PUG

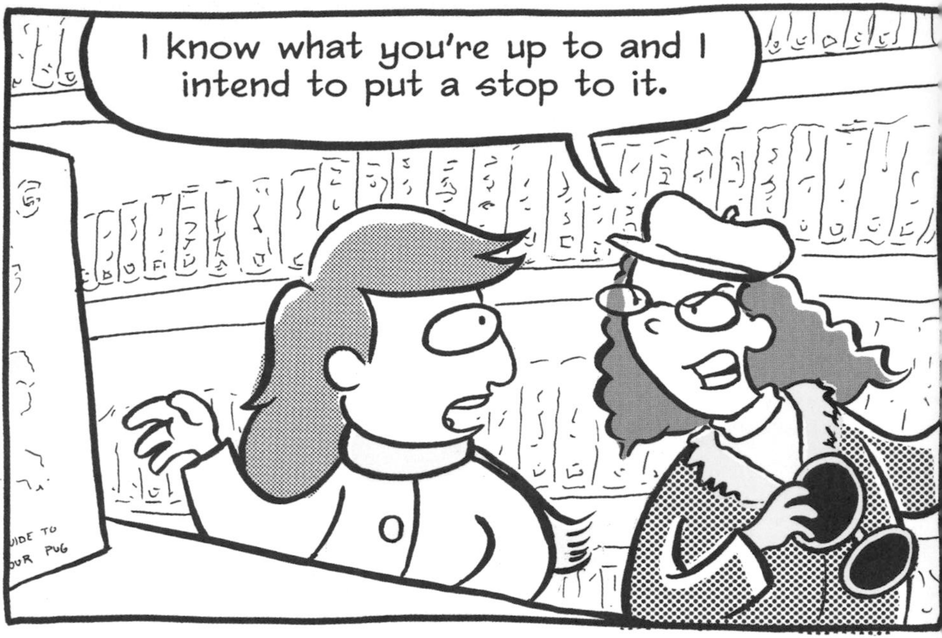
I know what you're up to and I intend to put a stop to it.

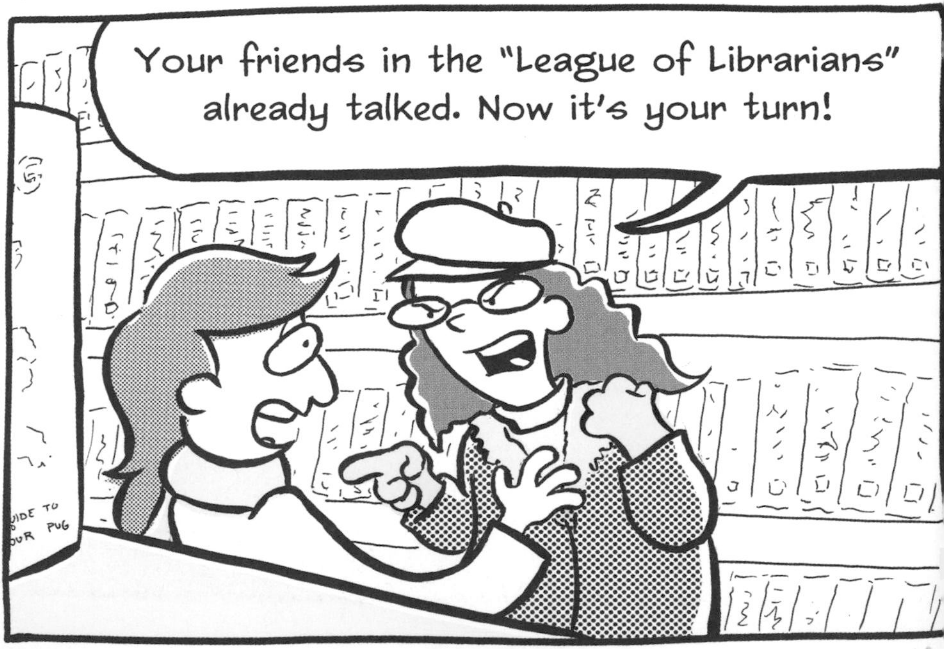
Your friends in the "League of Librarians" already talked. Now it's your turn!

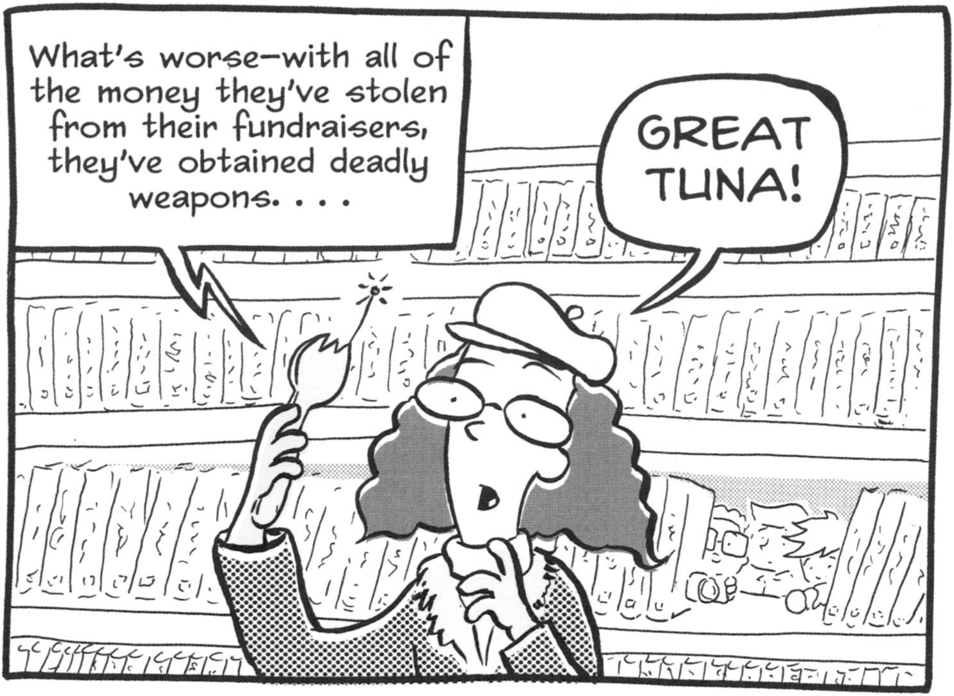
What's worse—with all of the money they've stolen from their fundraisers, they've obtained deadly weapons. . . .
GREAT TUNA!

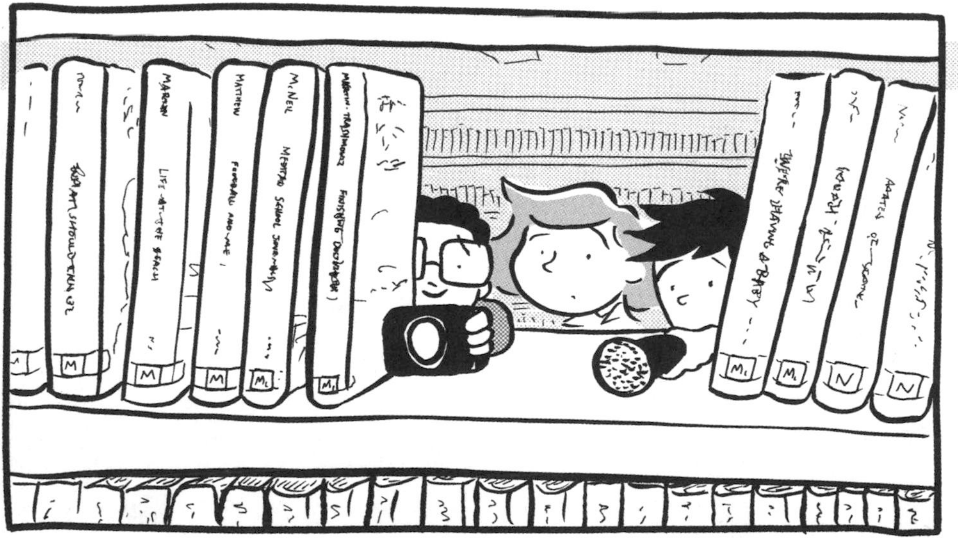

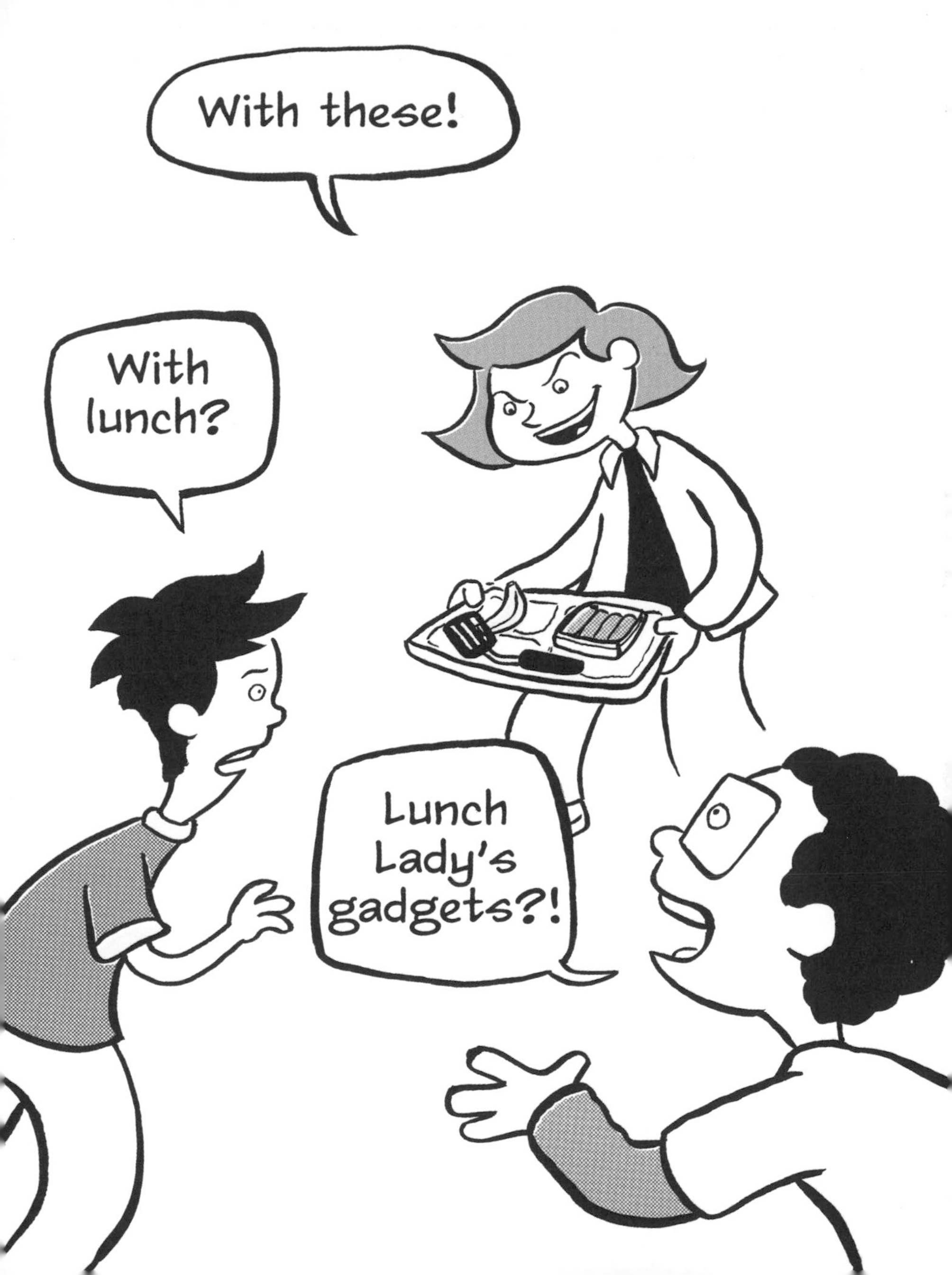
With these!
With lunch?
Lunch Lady's gadgets?!

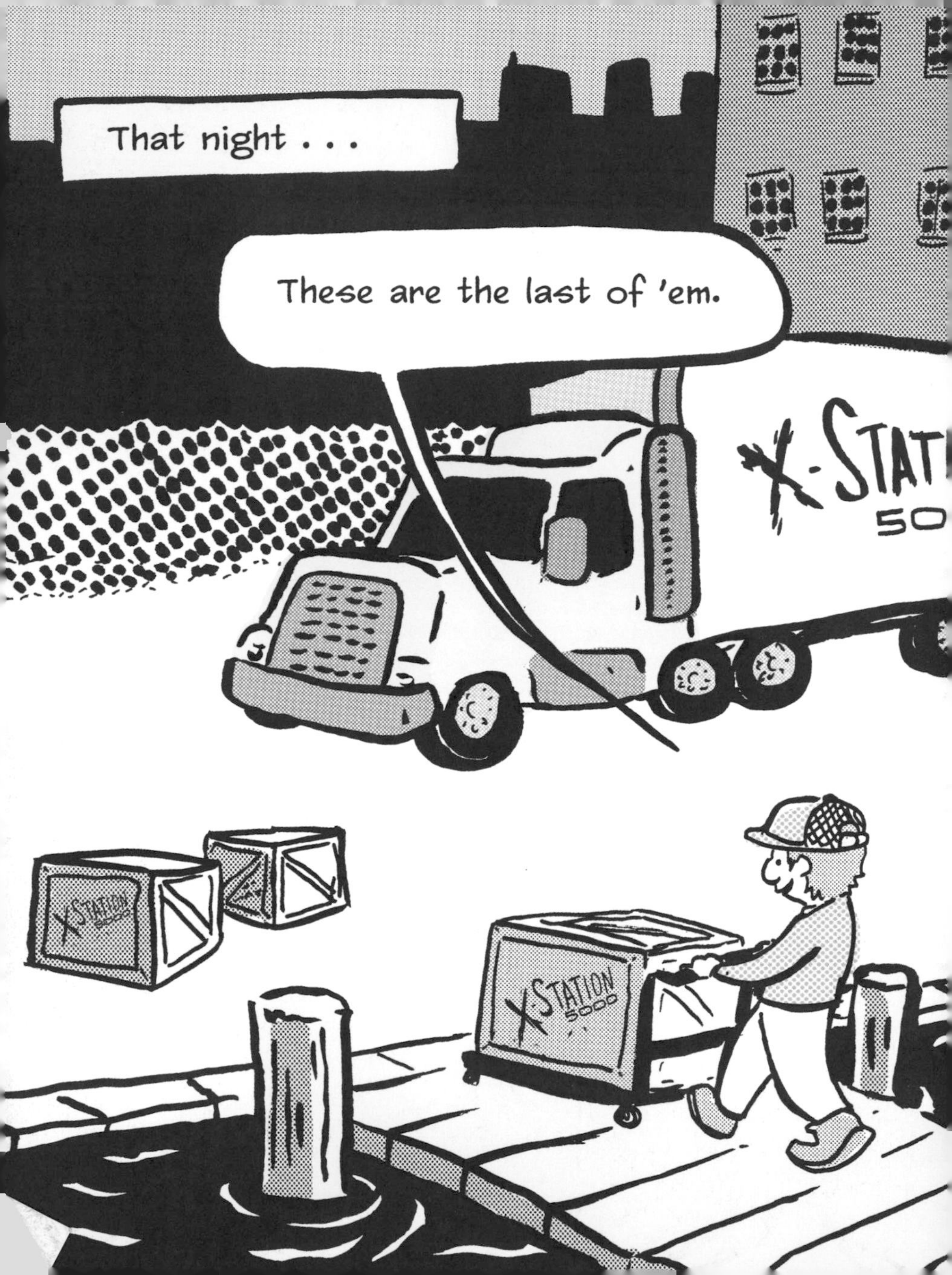
That night . . .
These are the last of 'em.
X-STAT
50
X-STATION 5000
X-STATION 5000

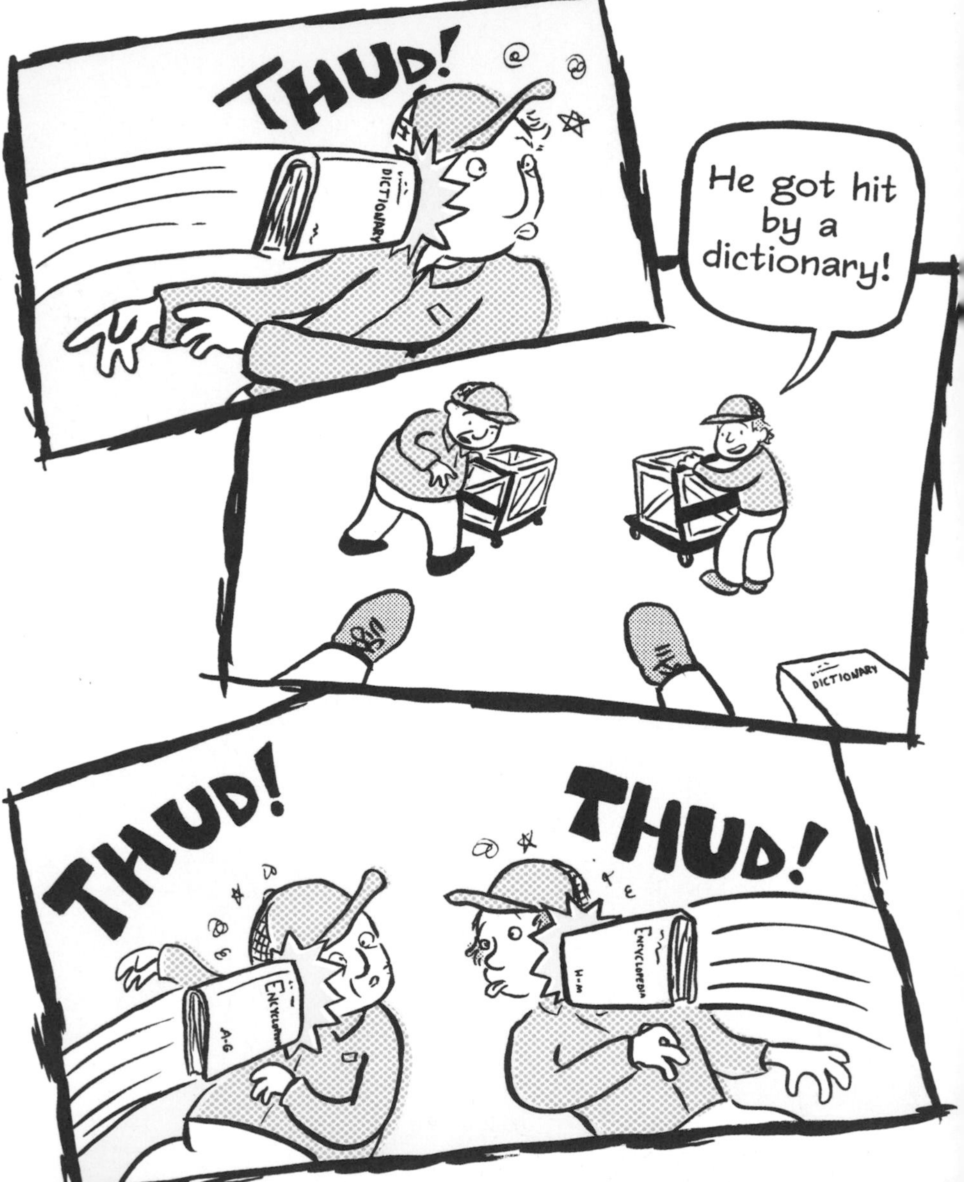
THUD!
DICTIONARY
He got hit by a dictionary!
DICTIONARY
THUD!
ENCYCLOPEDIA
A-G
THUD!
ENCYCLOPEDIA
H-M

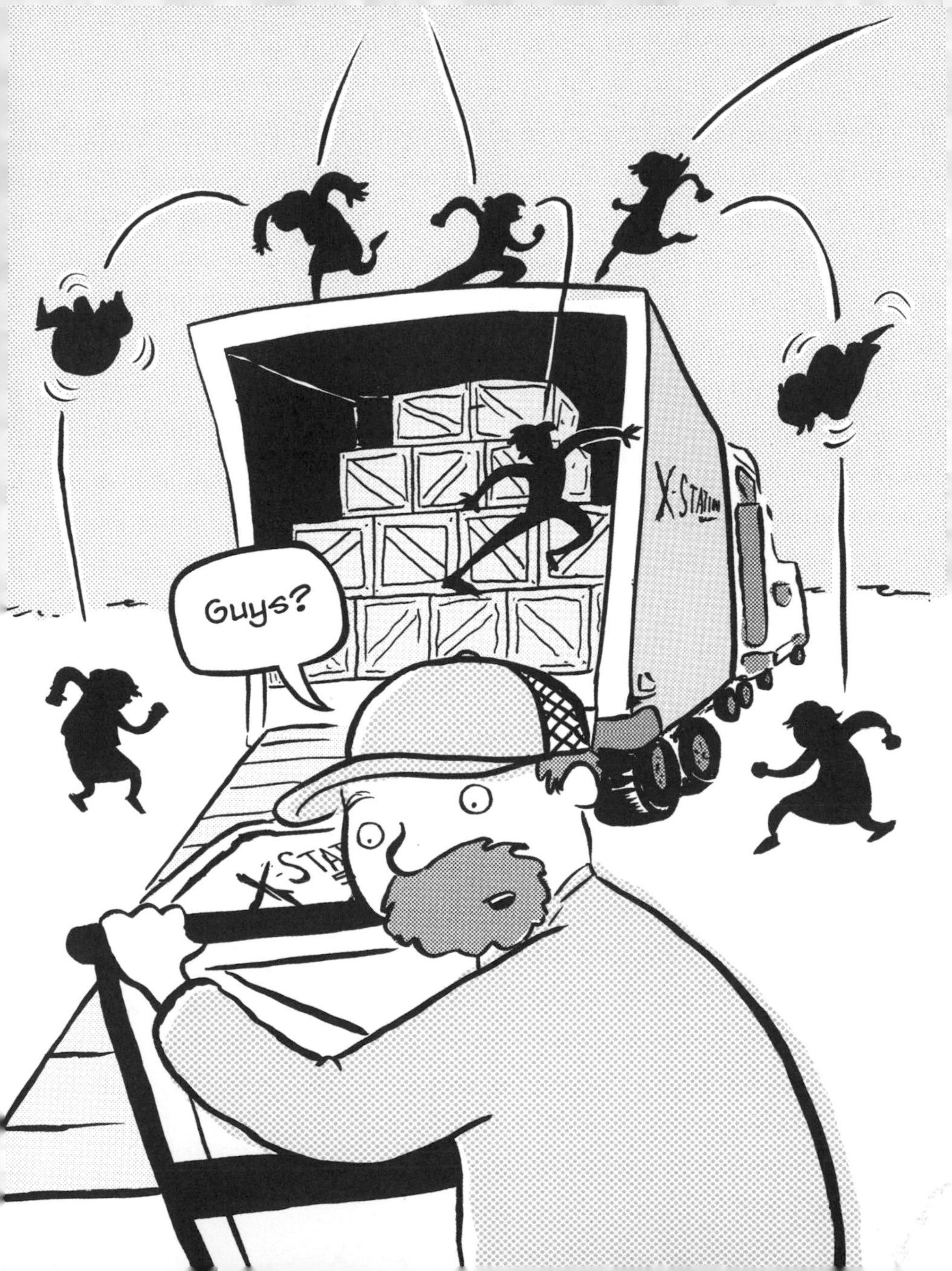
Guys?

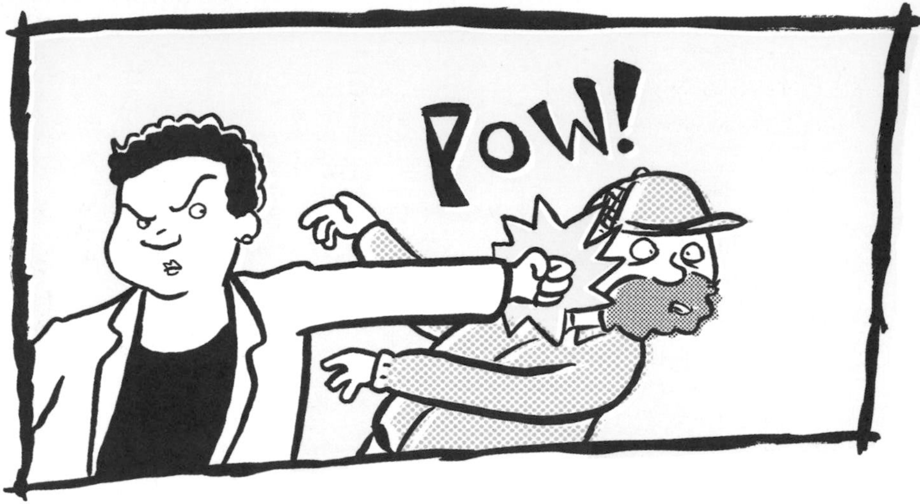
POW!

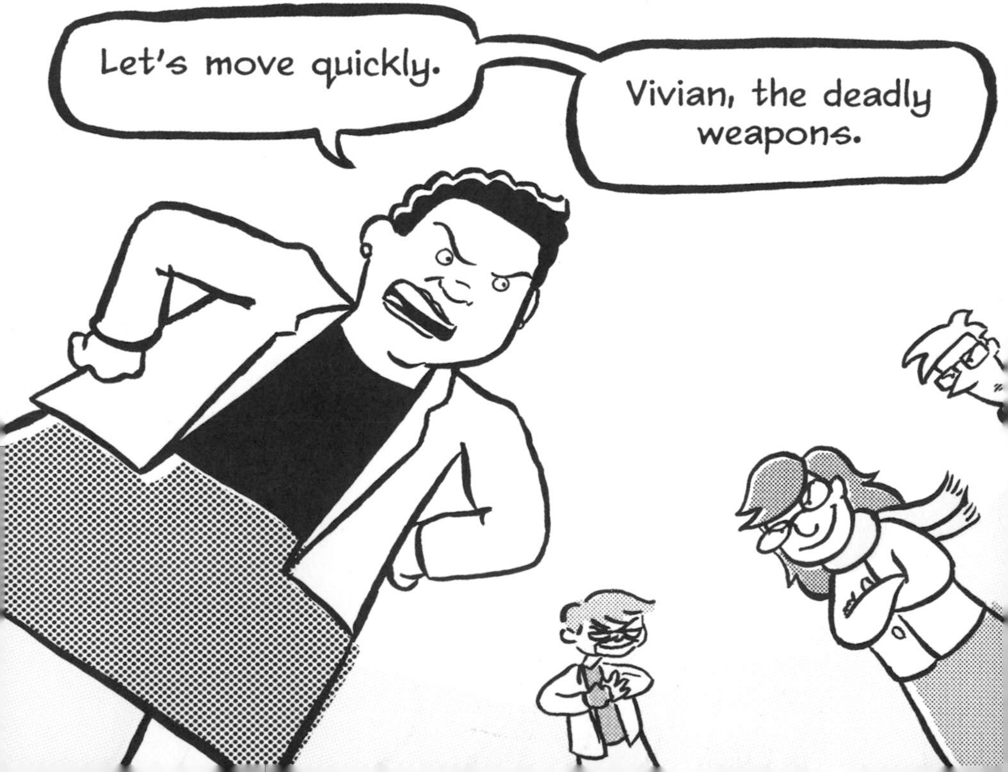
Let's move quickly.
Vivian, the deadly weapons.

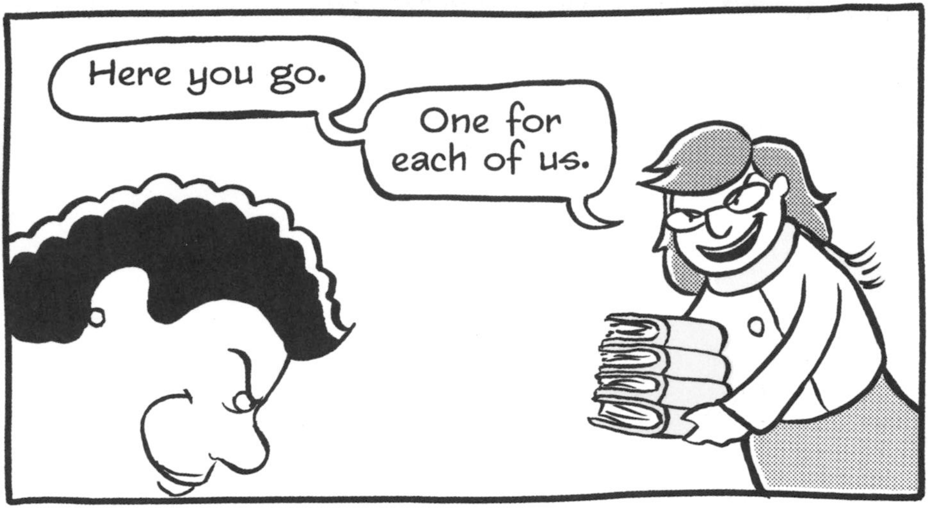
Here you go.
One for each of us.

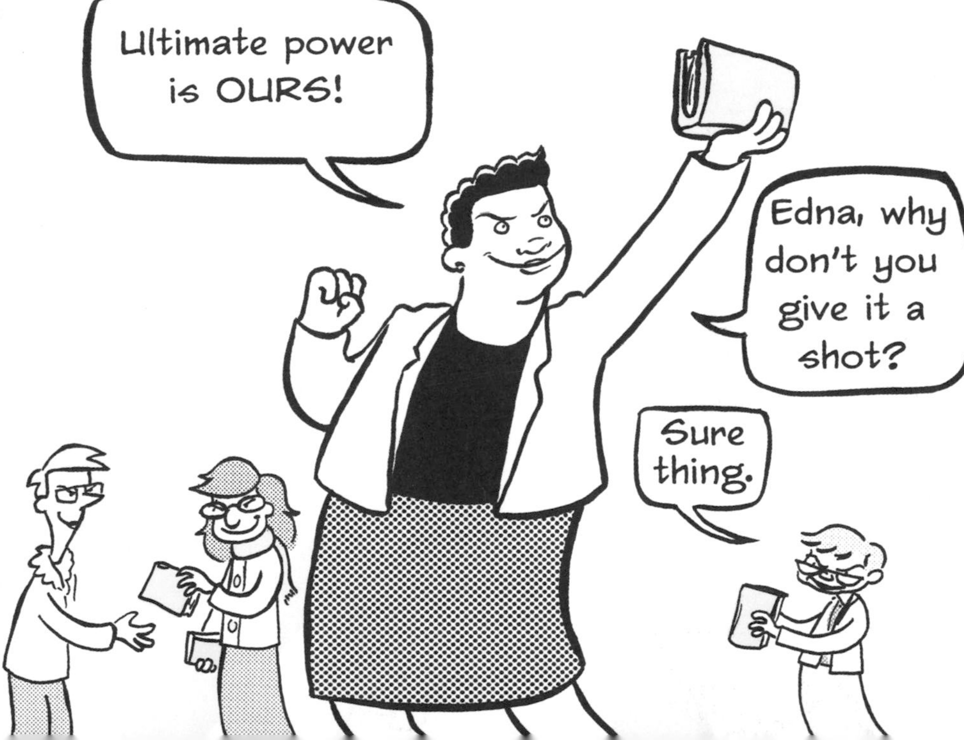
Ultimate power is OURS!
Edna, why don't you give it a shot?
Sure thing.

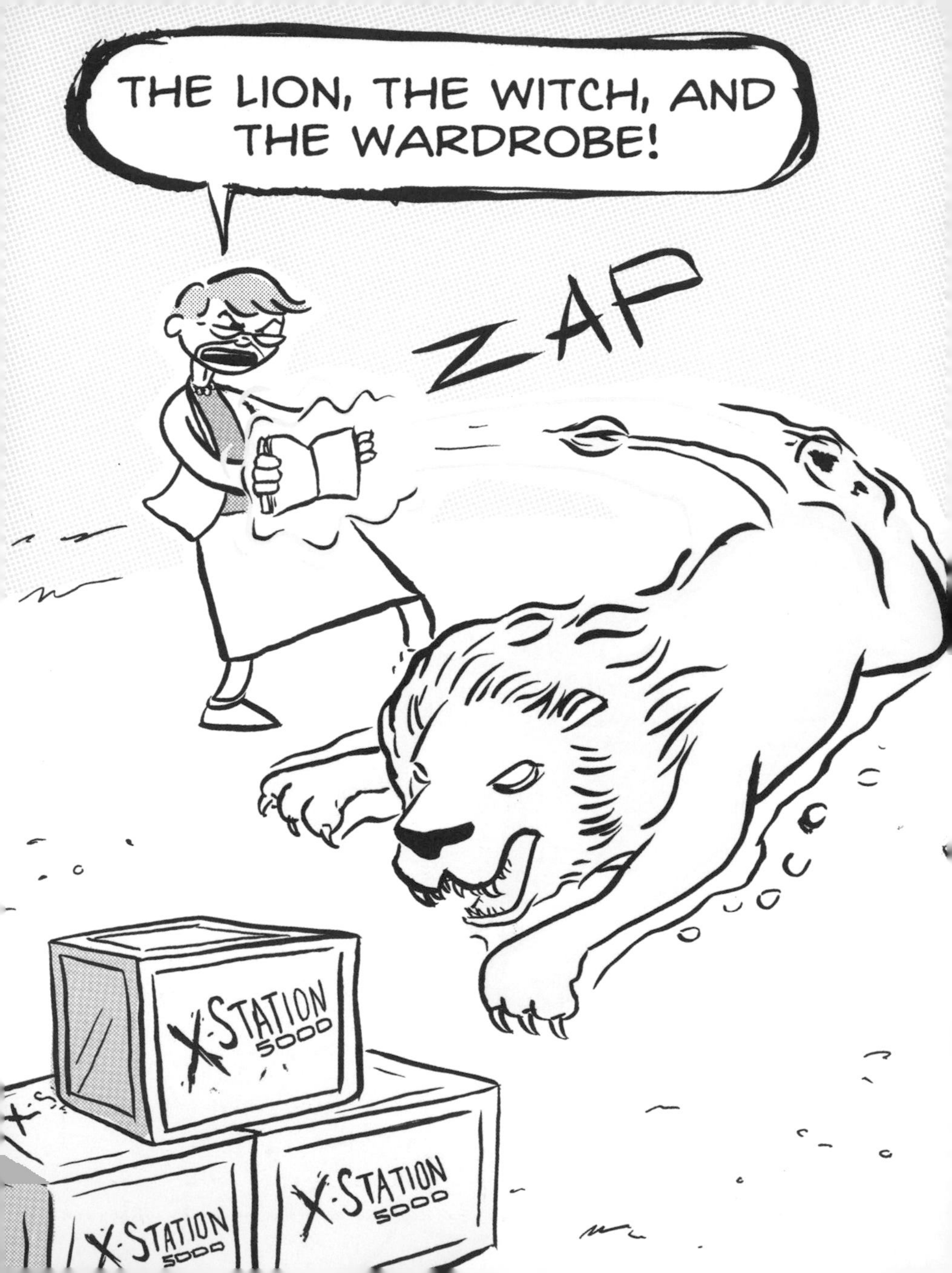
THE LION, THE WITCH, AND THE WARDROBE!
ZAP
X-STATION 5000
X-STATION 5000
X-STATION 5000

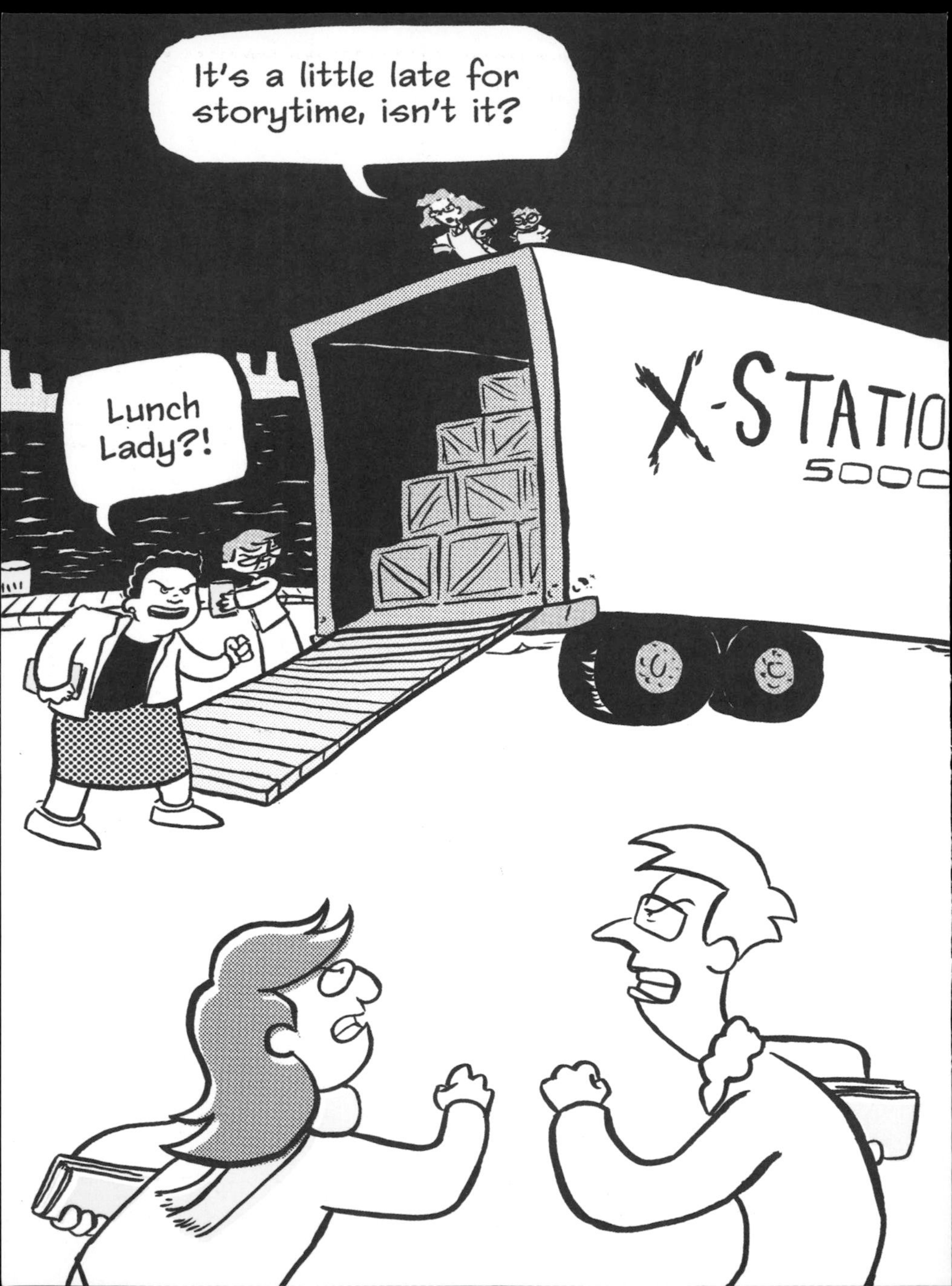
It's a little late for storytime, isn't it?
Lunch Lady?!
X-STATIO
5000

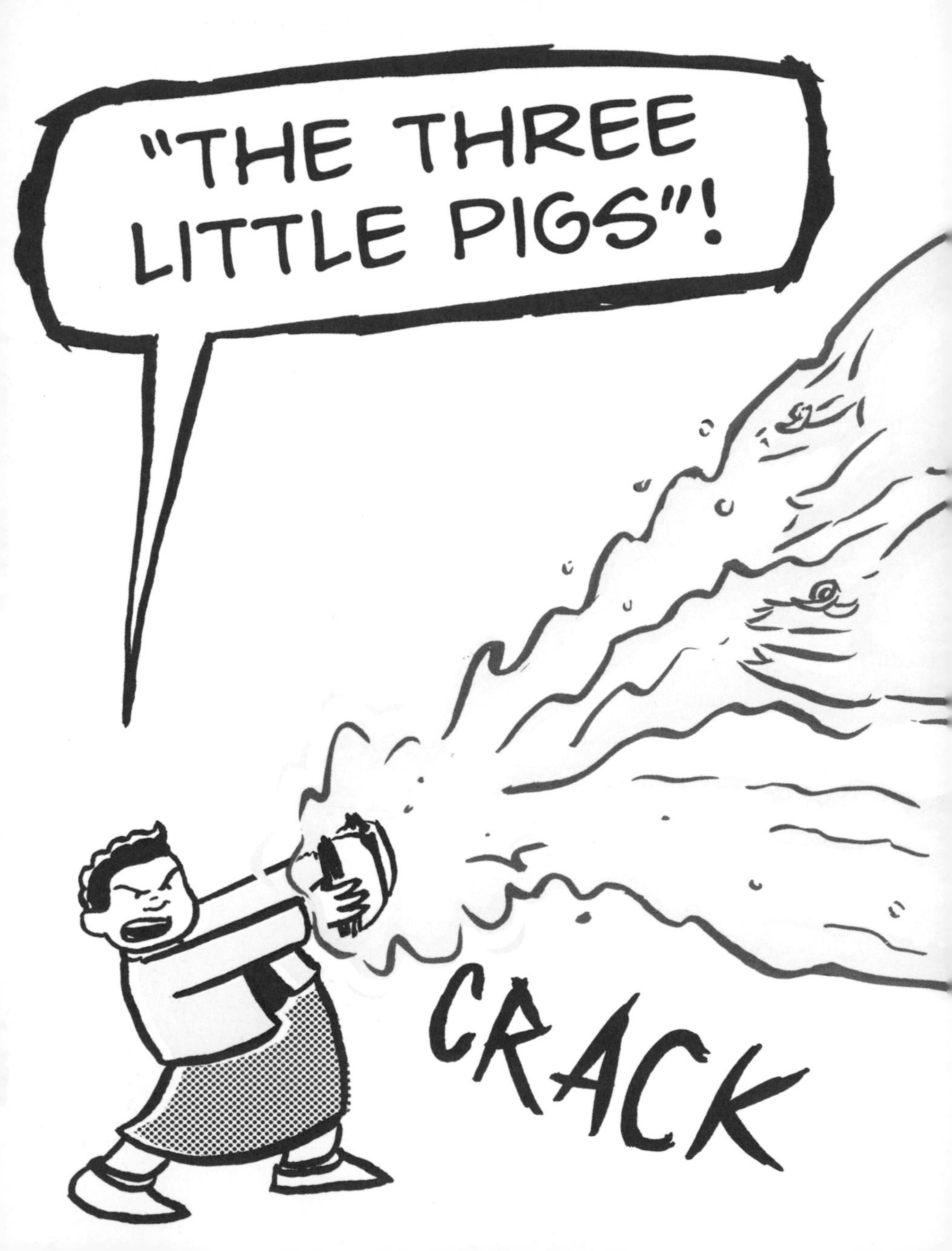
"THE THREE LITTLE PIGS"!
CRACK

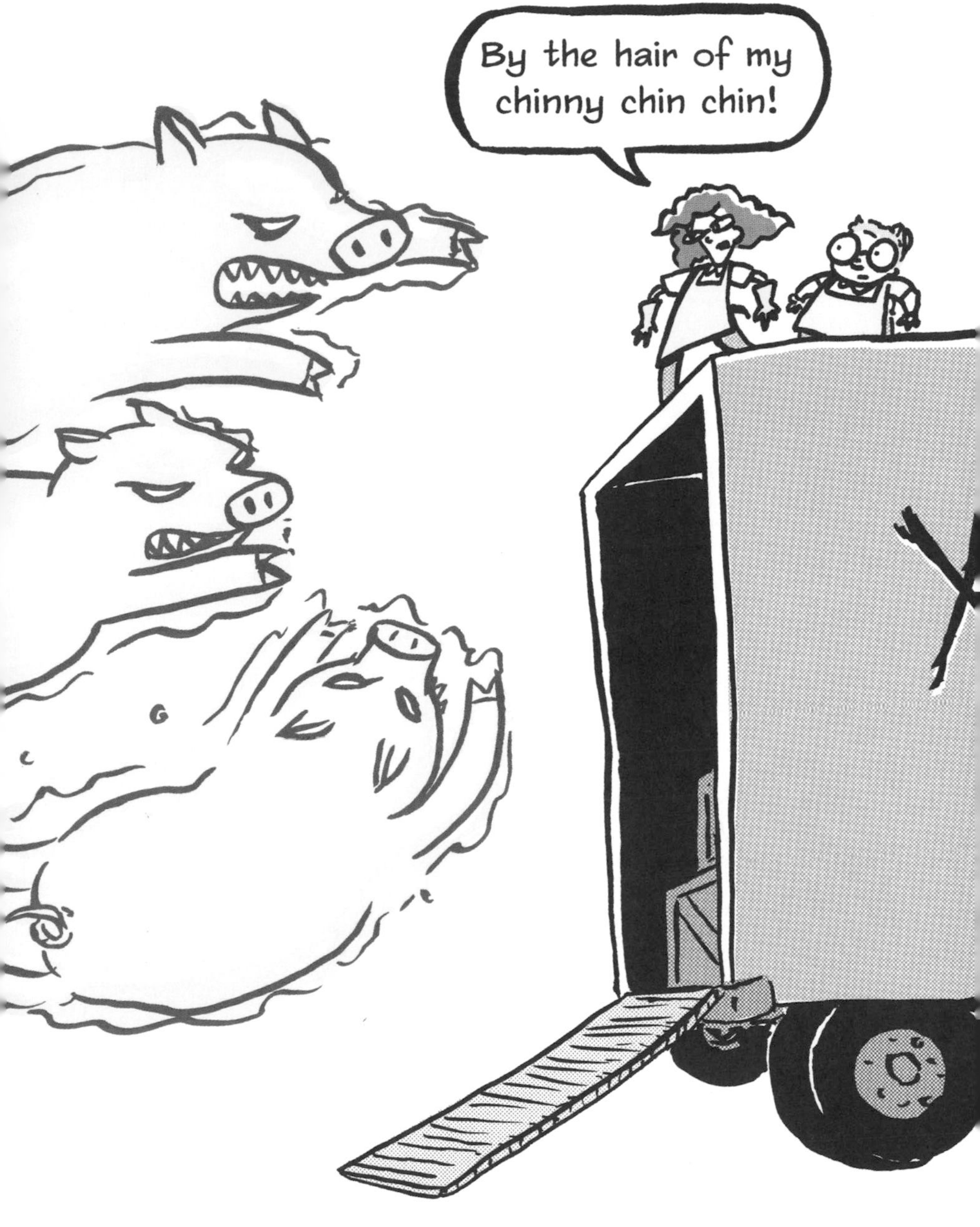
By the hair of my chinny chin chin!

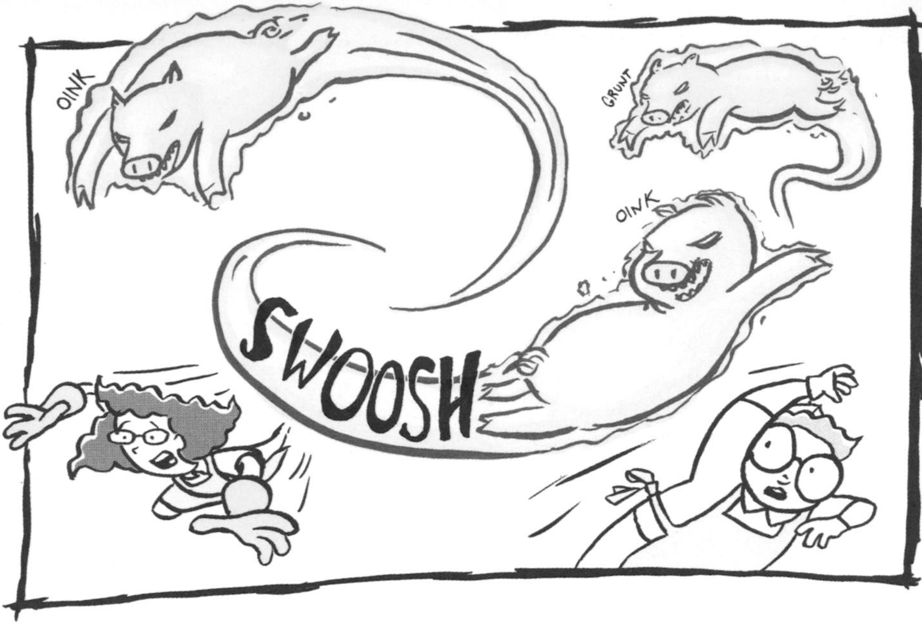
OINK
GRUNT
OINK
SWOOSH

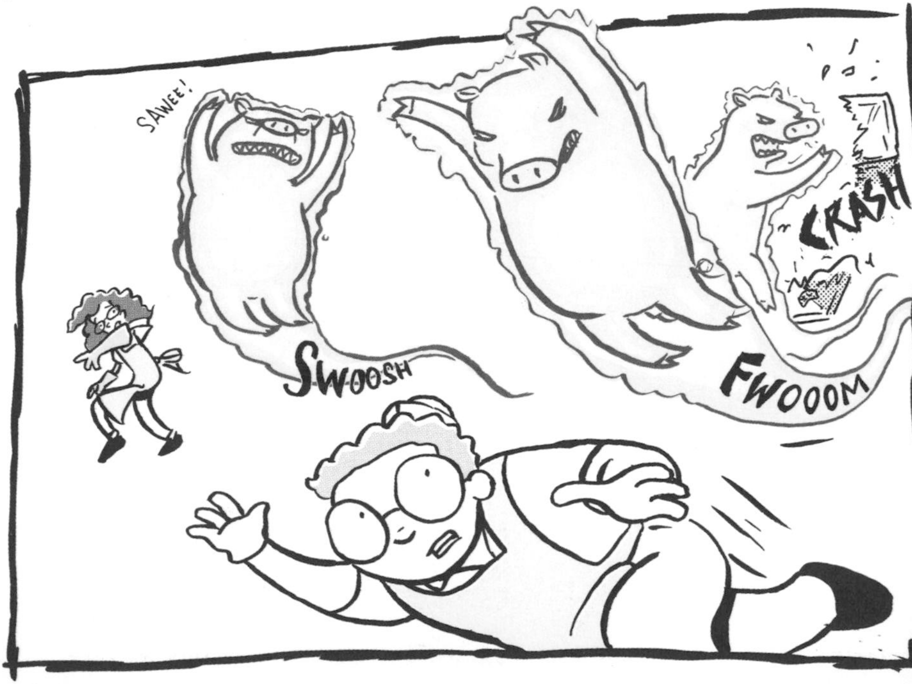
SAWEE!
CRASH
SWOOSH
FWOOOM

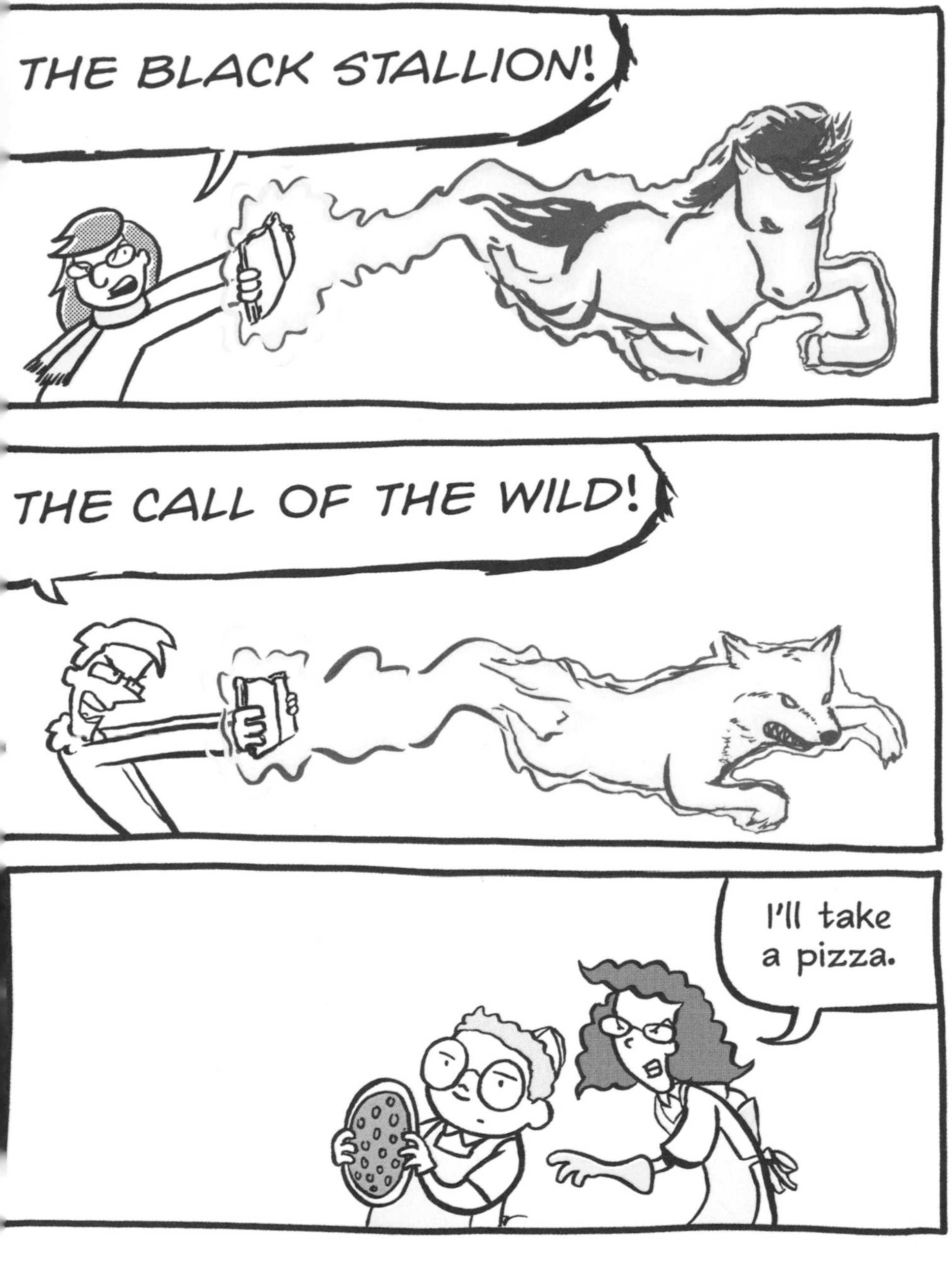
THE BLACK STALLION!
THE CALL OF THE WILD!
I'll take a pizza.

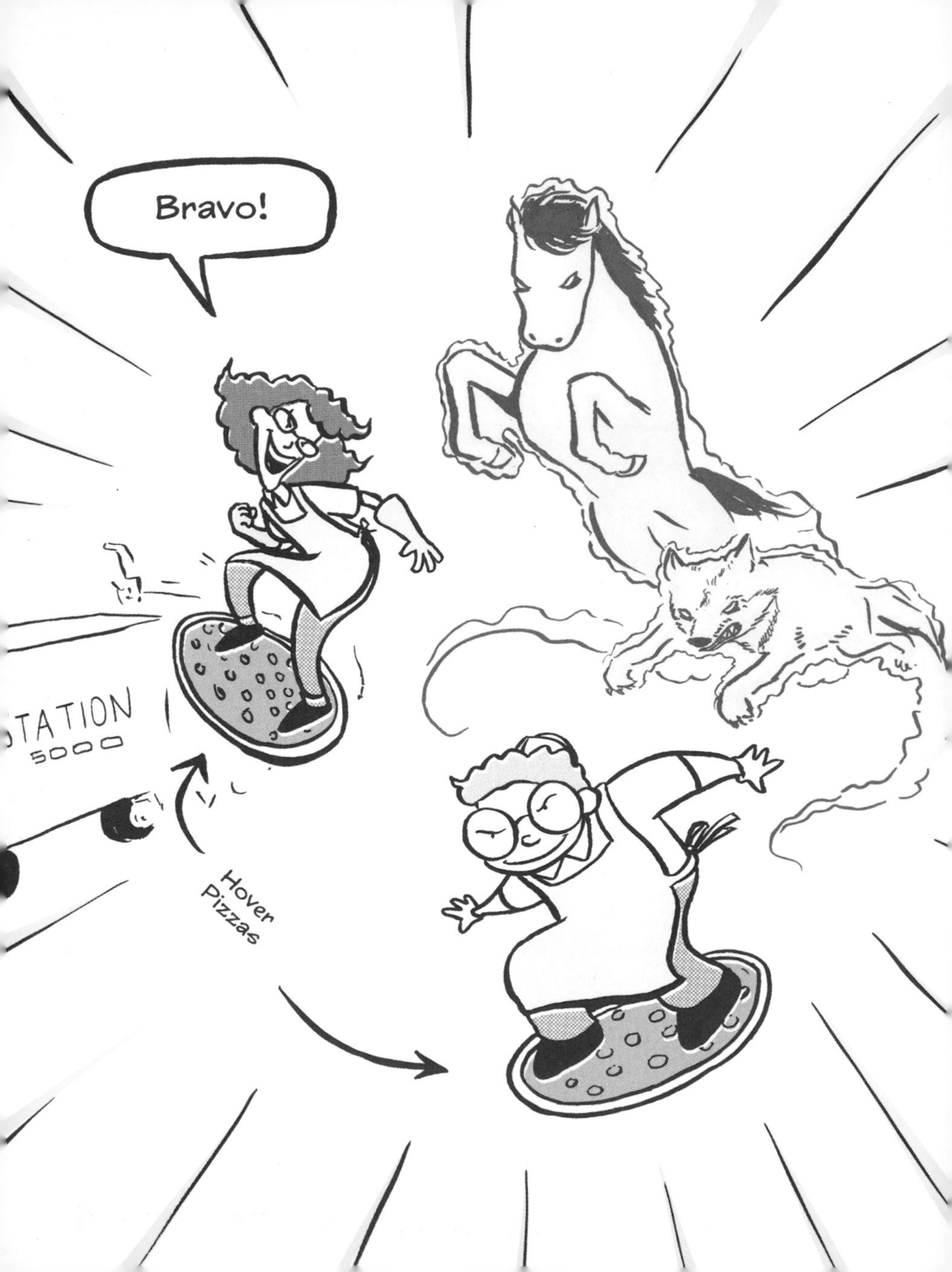
Bravo!
STATION
5000
Hover Pizzas

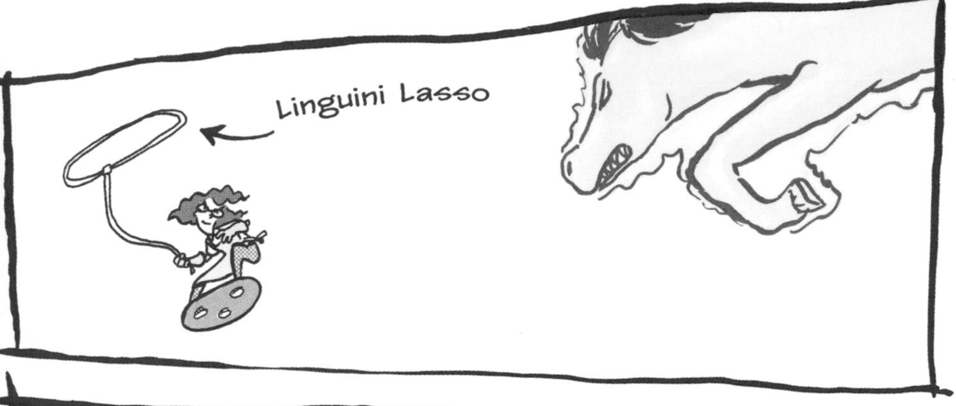
Linguini Lasso

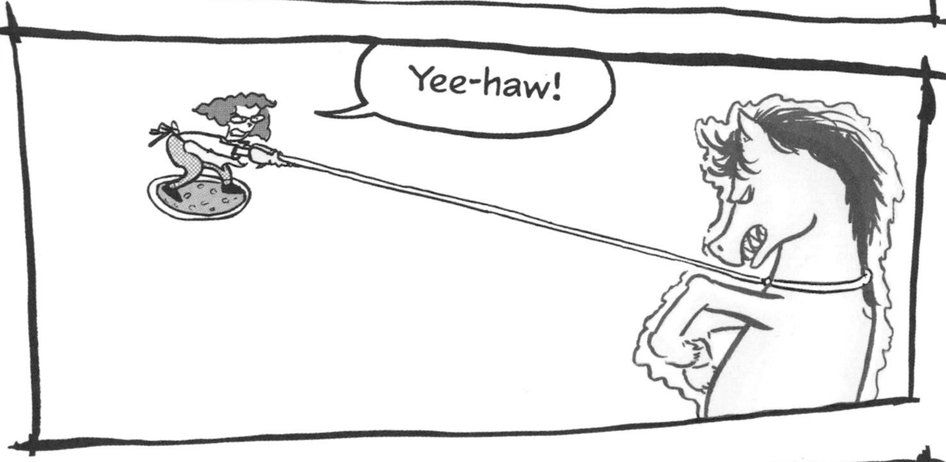
Yee-haw!

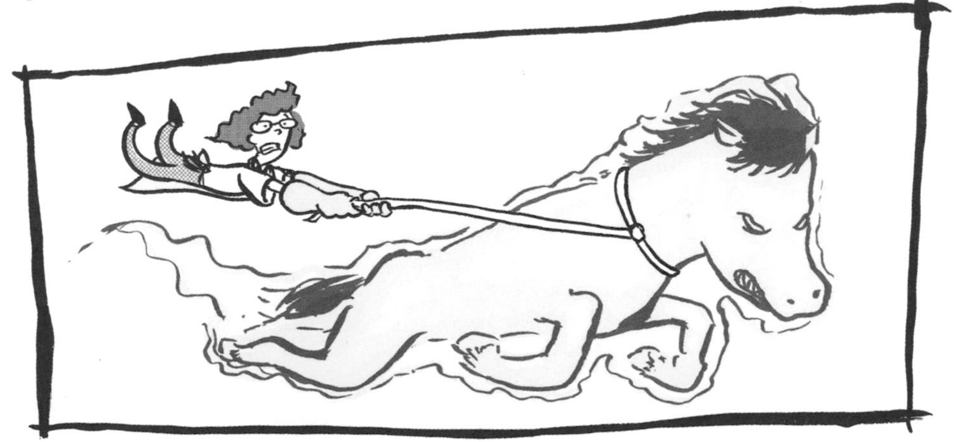

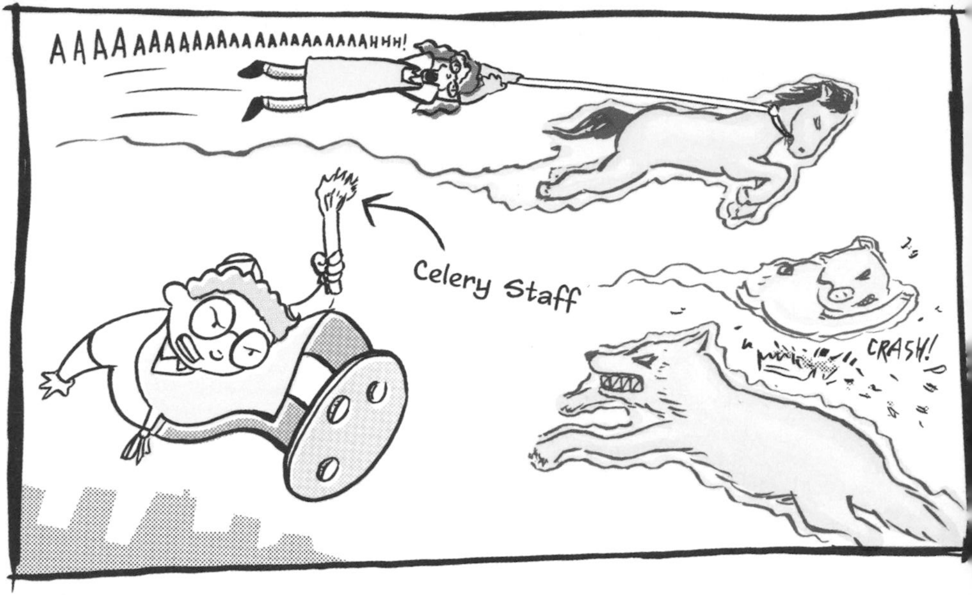
AAAAAAAAAAAAAAAAAAAAAAAAAHHH!
Celery Staff
CRASH!

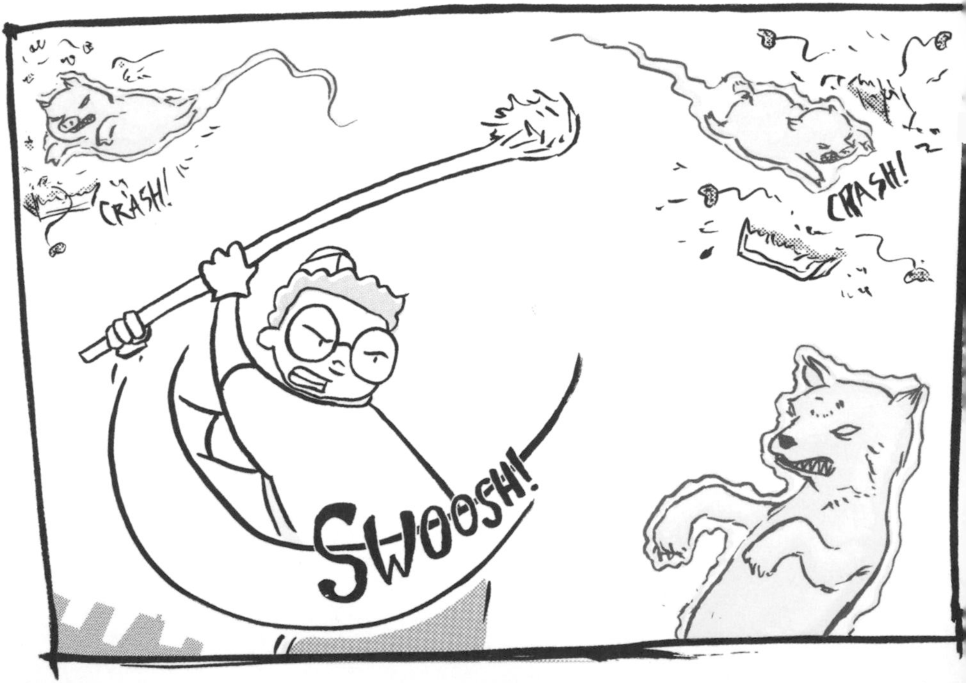
CRASH!
CRASH!
SWOOSH!

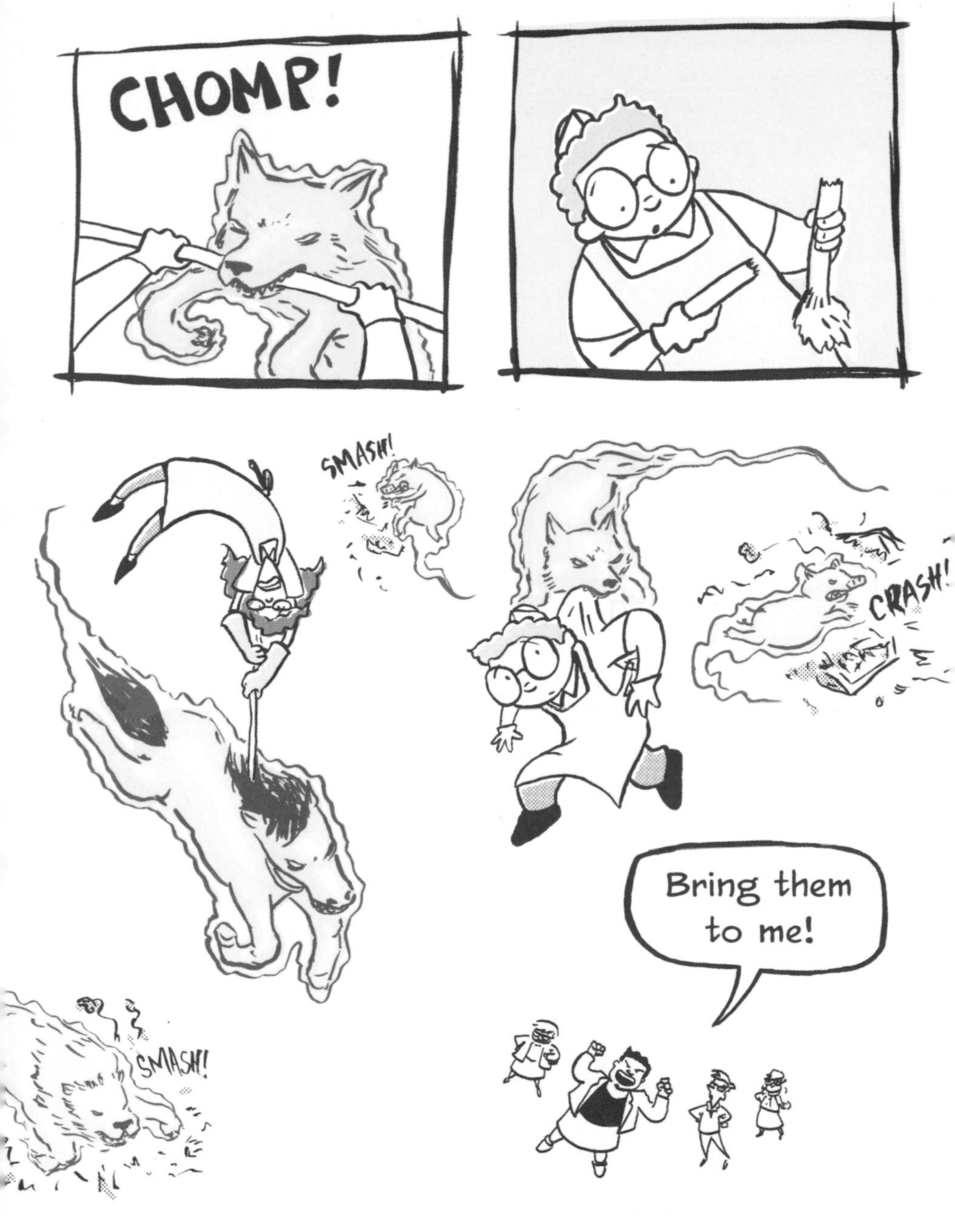
CHOMP!
SMASH!
CRASH!
Bring them to me!
SMASH!

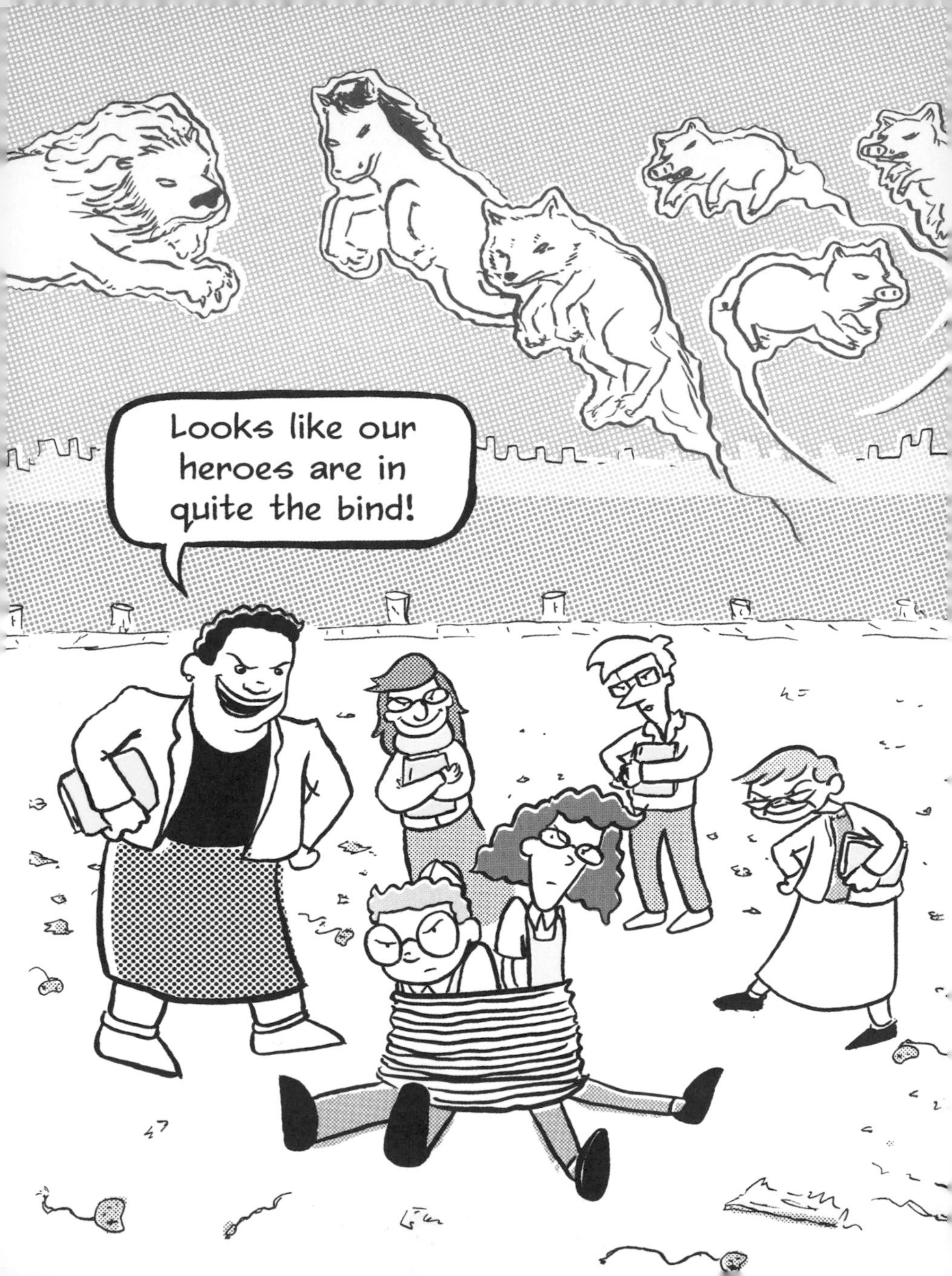
Looks like our heroes are in quite the bind!

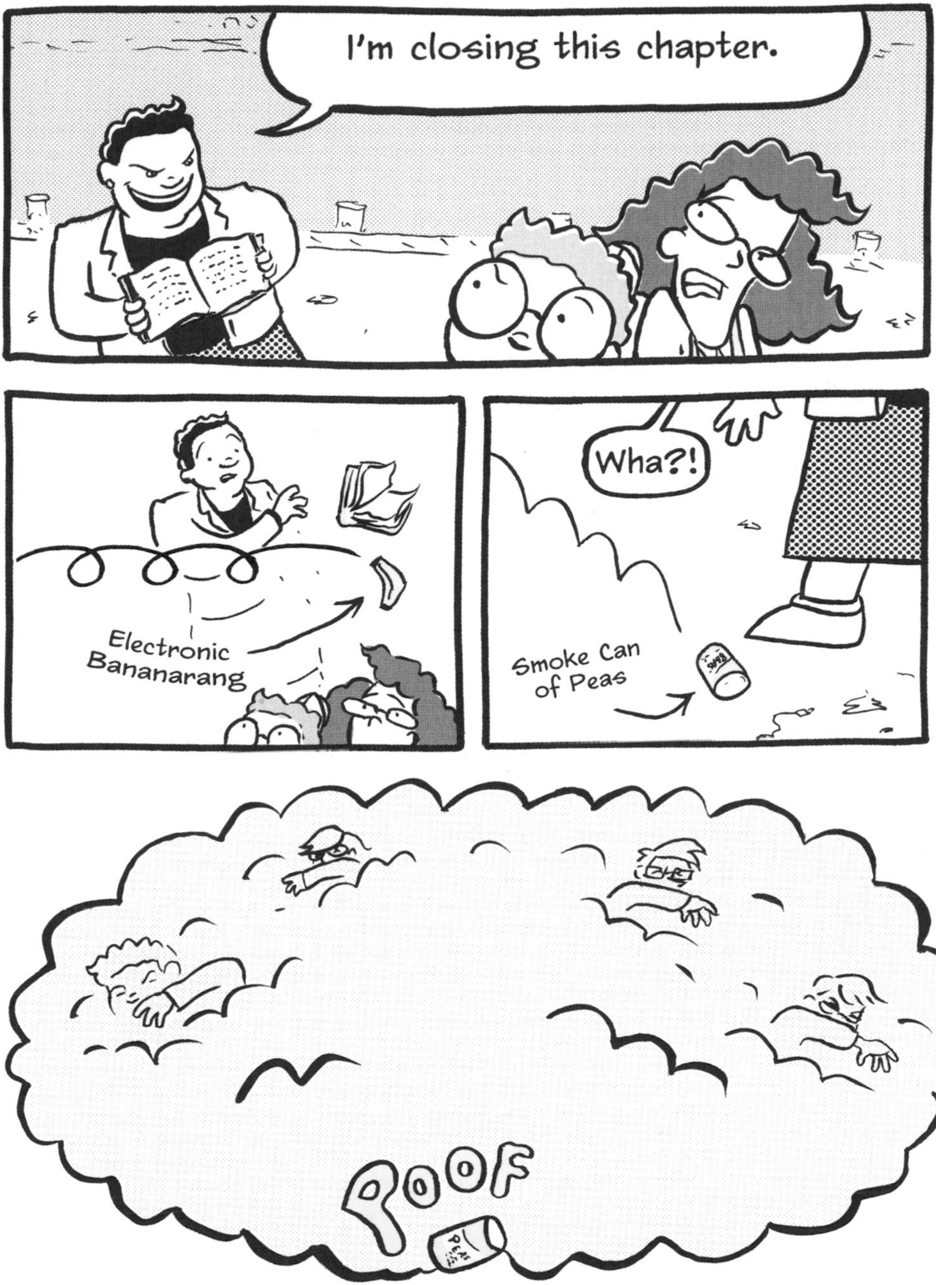
I'm closing this chapter.
Electronic Bananarang
Wha?!
Smoke Can of Peas
POOF

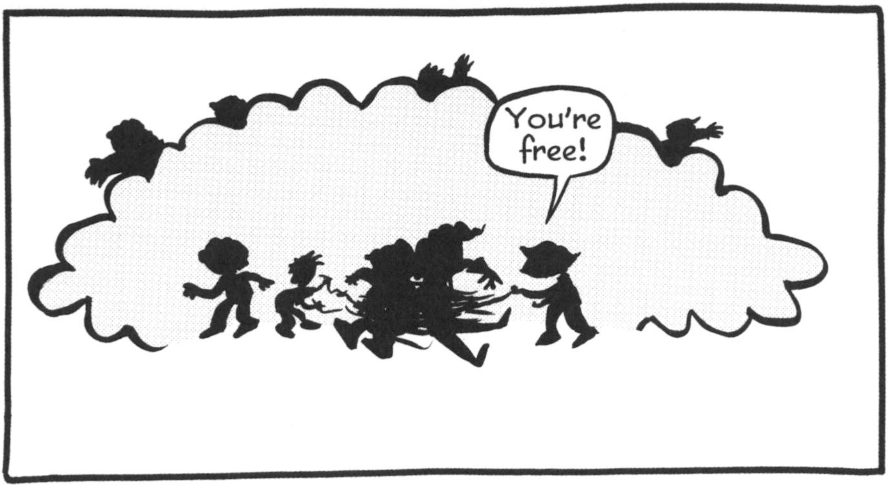
You're free!

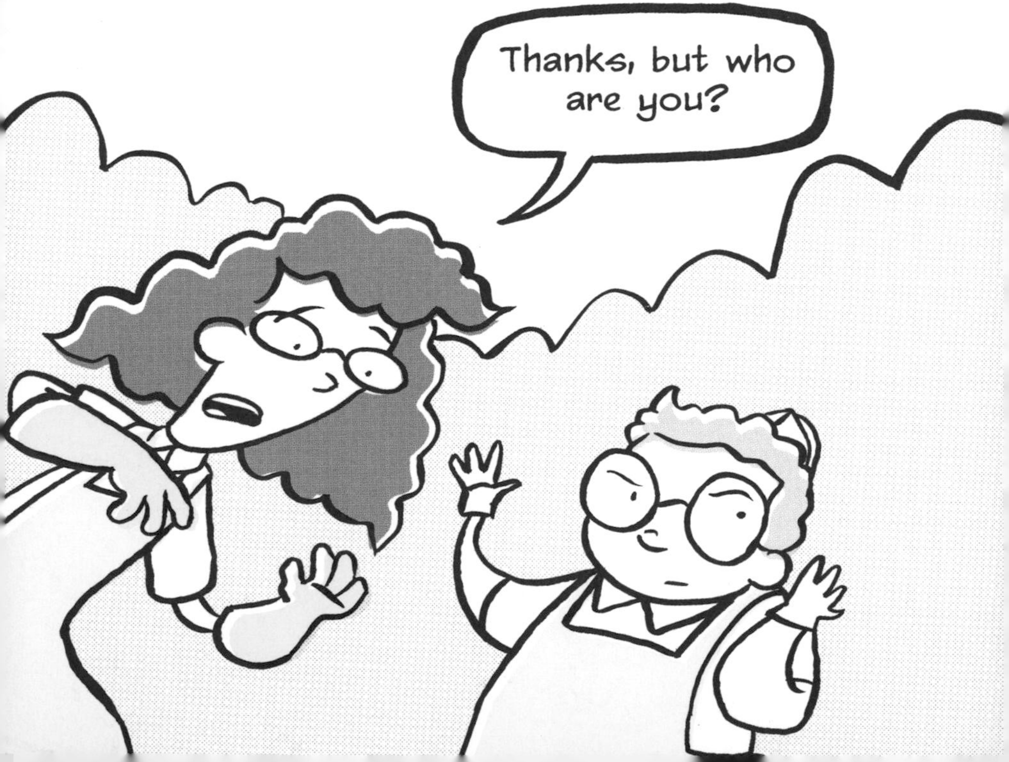
Thanks, but who are you?

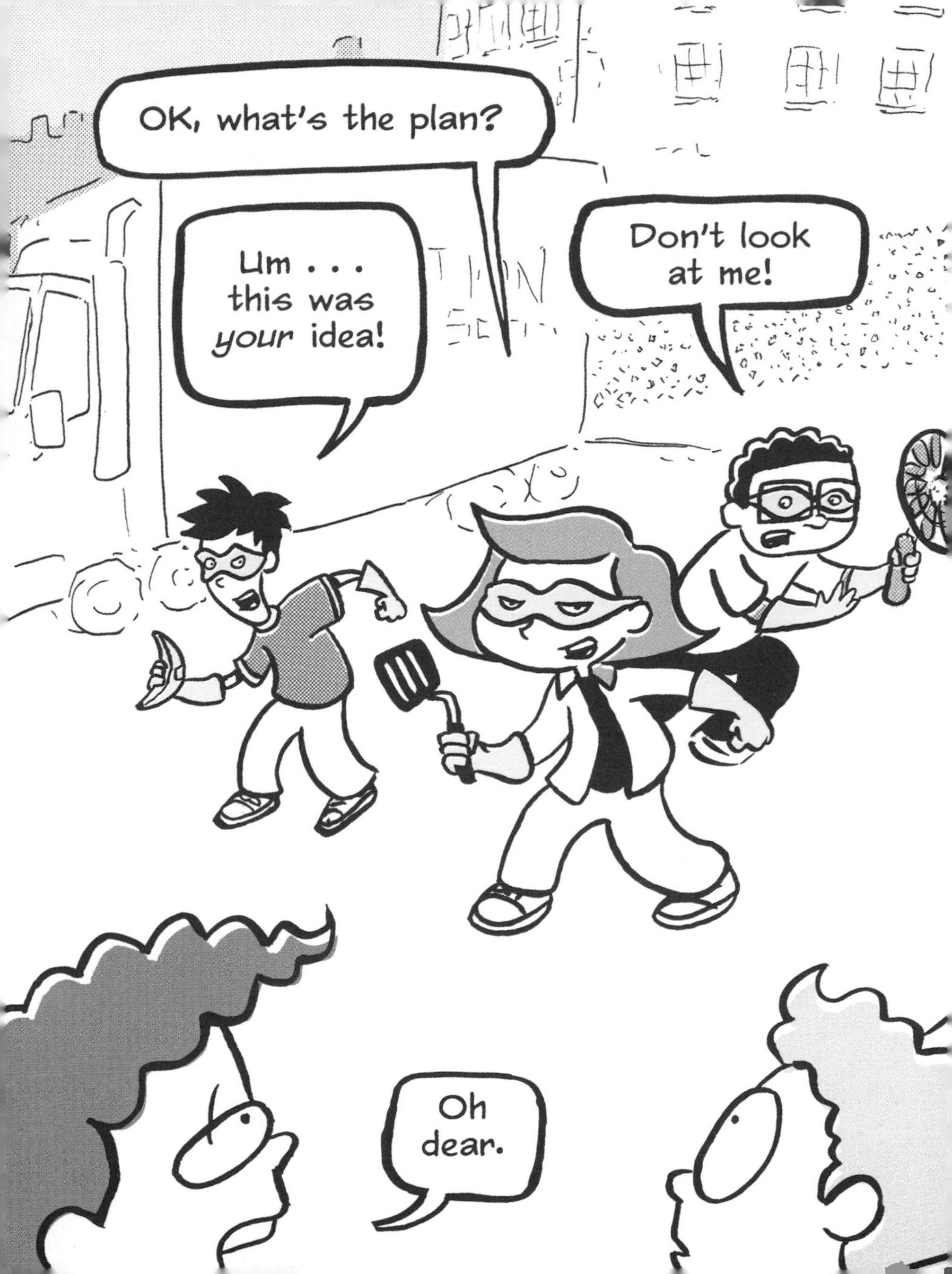

OK, what's the plan?
Um . . . this was *your* idea!
Don't look at me!
Oh dear.

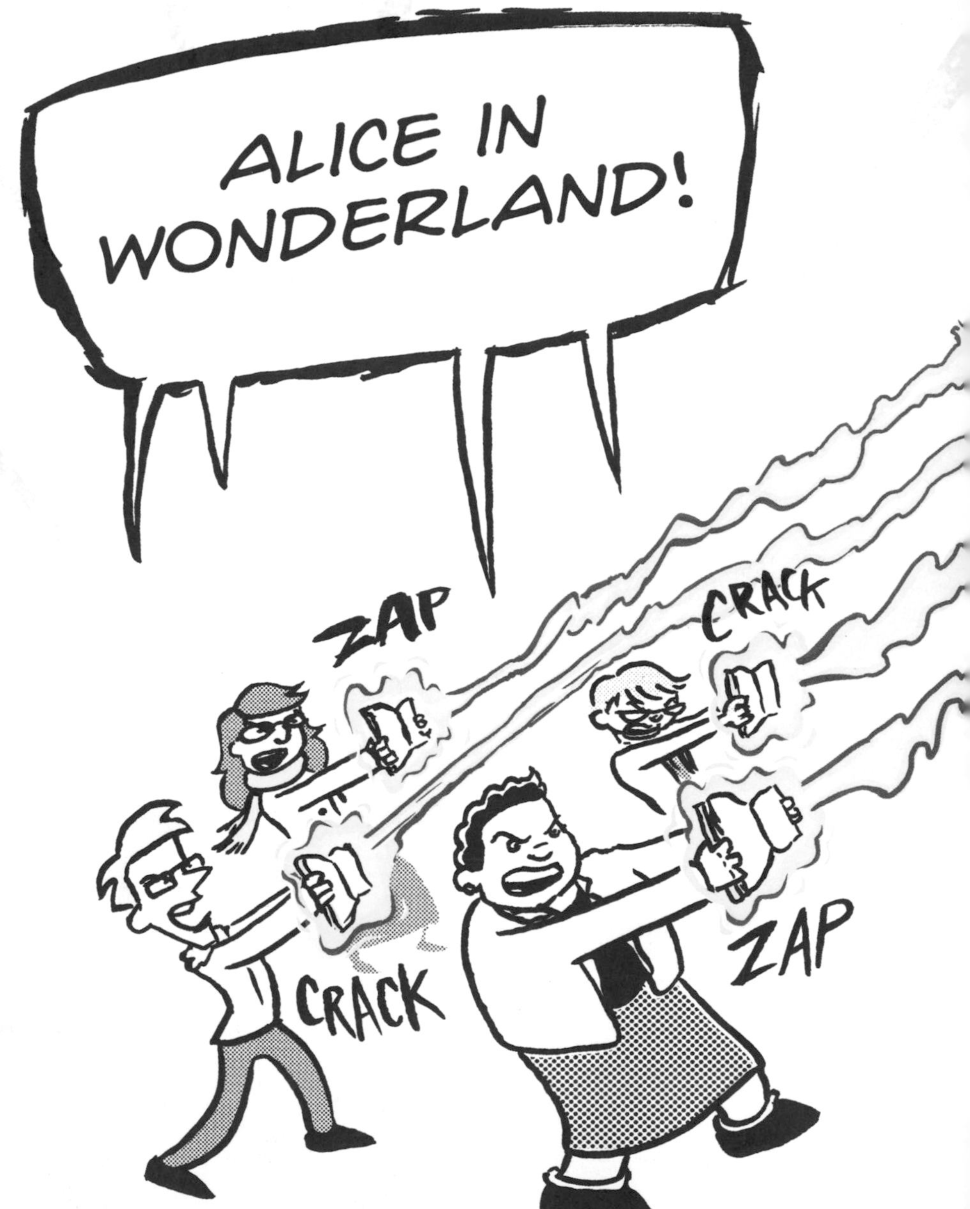

ALICE IN WONDERLAND!
ZAP
CRACK
CRACK
ZAP

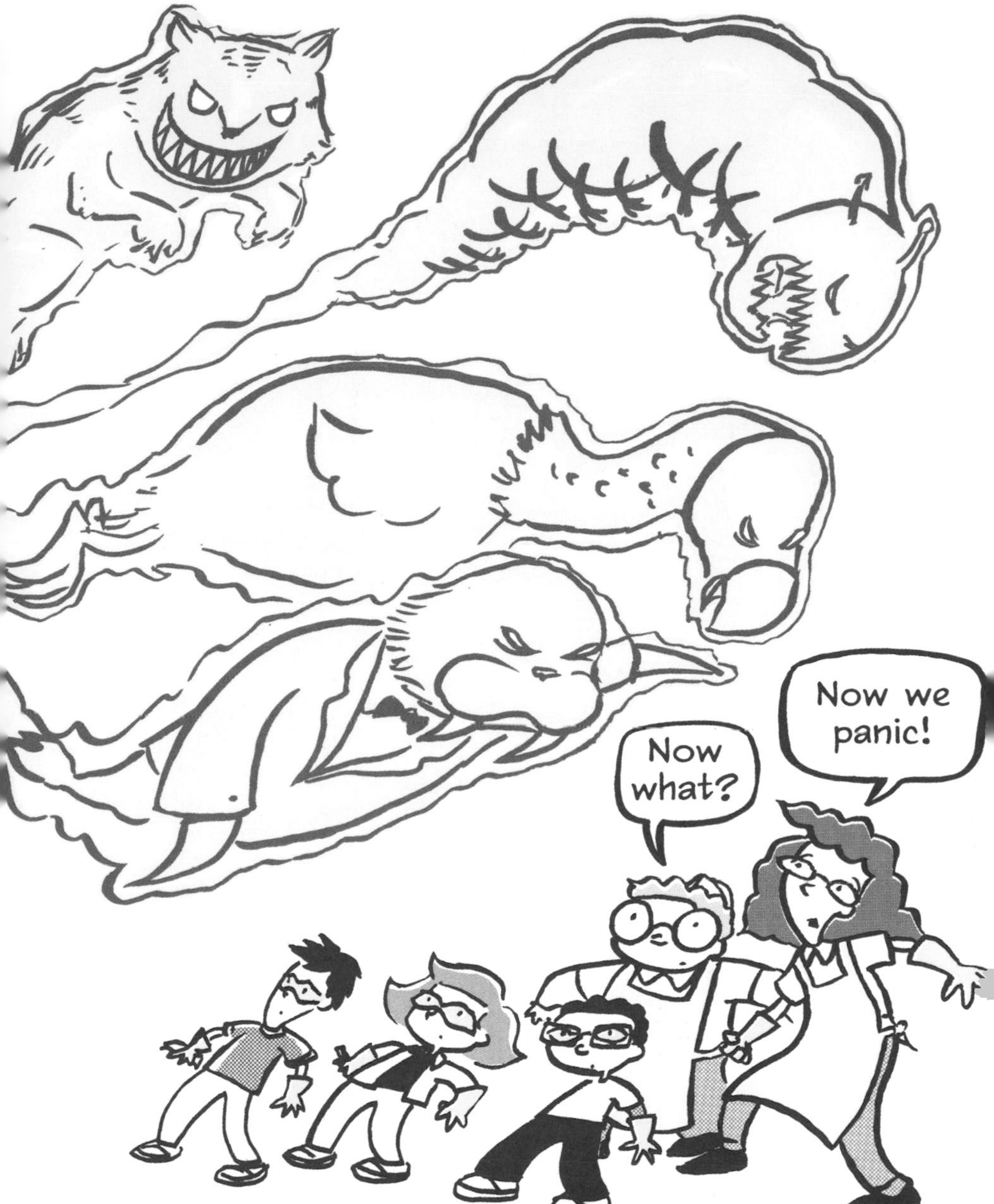
Now what?
Now we panic!

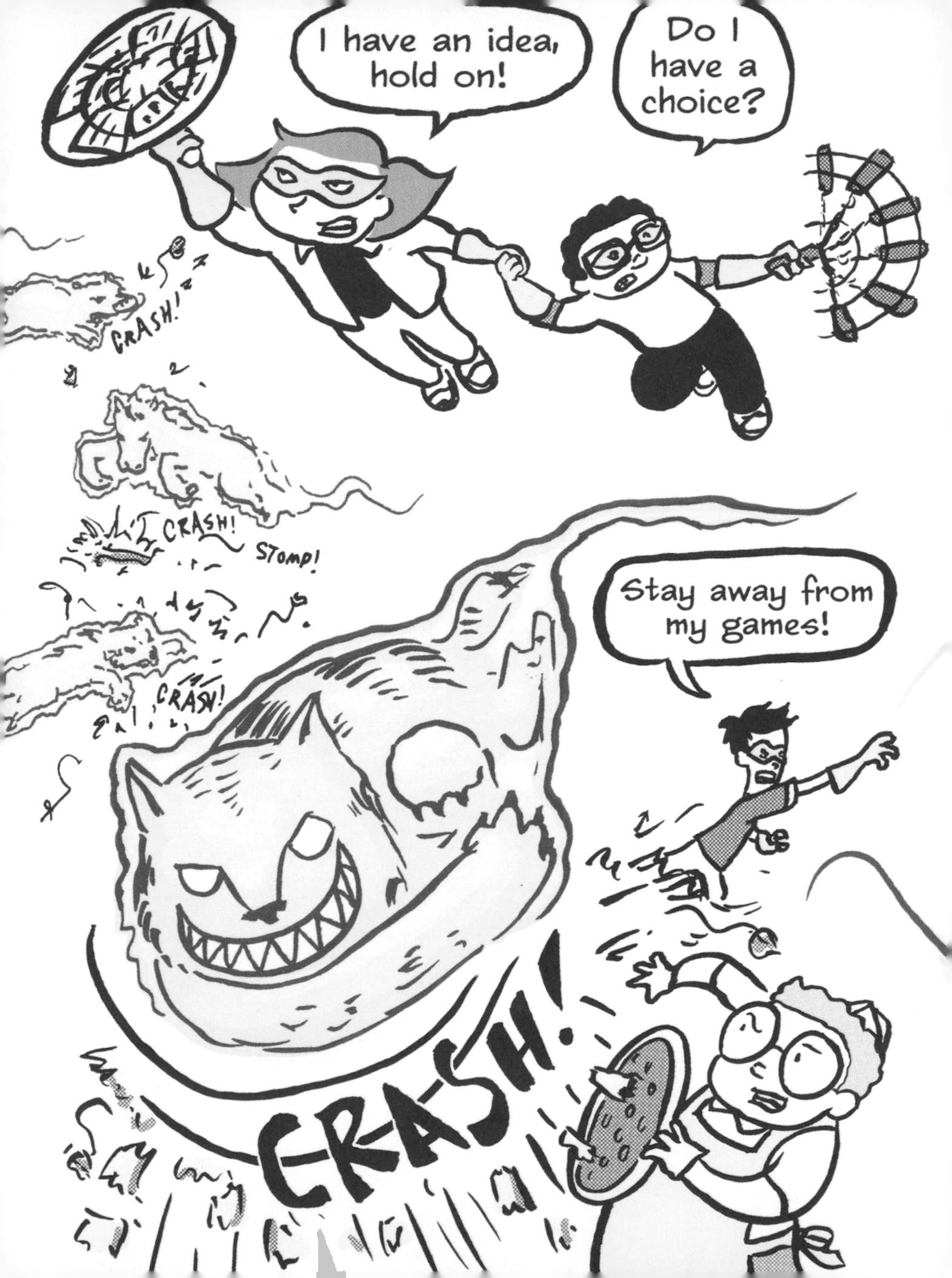
I have an idea, hold on!
Do I have a choice?
CRASH!
CRASH!
STOMP!
CRASH!
Stay away from my games!
CRASH!

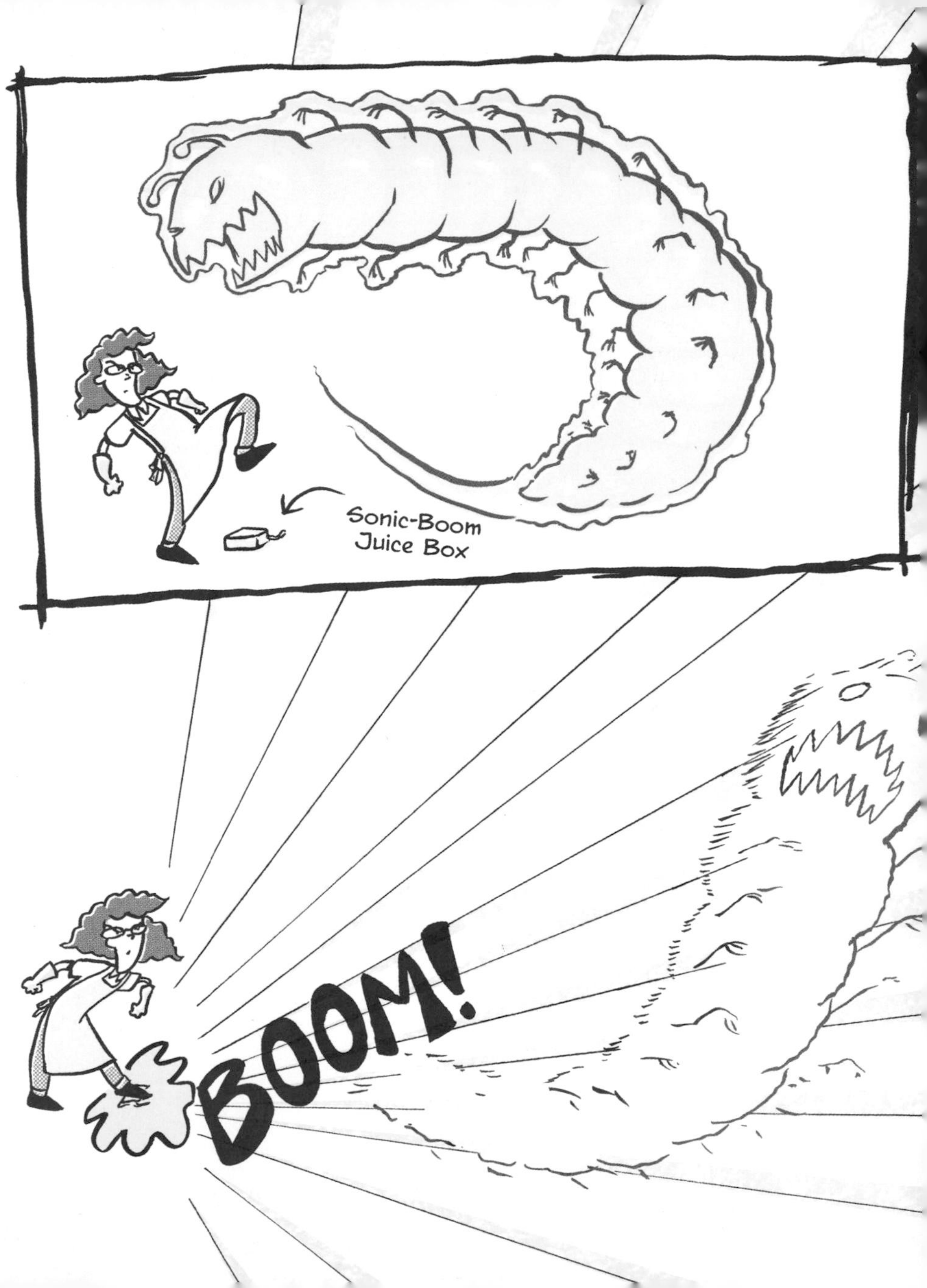
Sonic-Boom
Juice Box
BOOM!

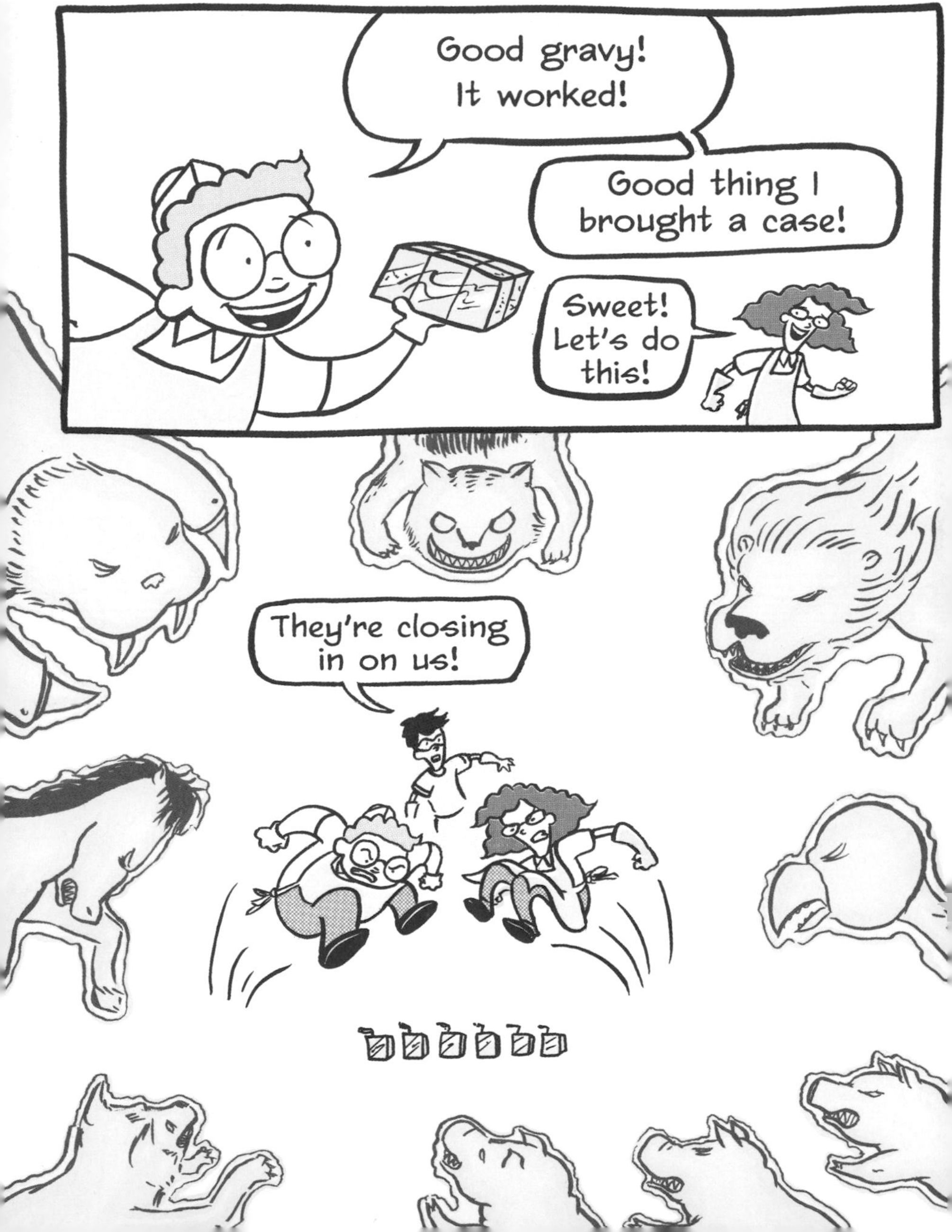
Good gravy! It worked!
Good thing I brought a case!
Sweet! Let's do this!
They're closing in on us!

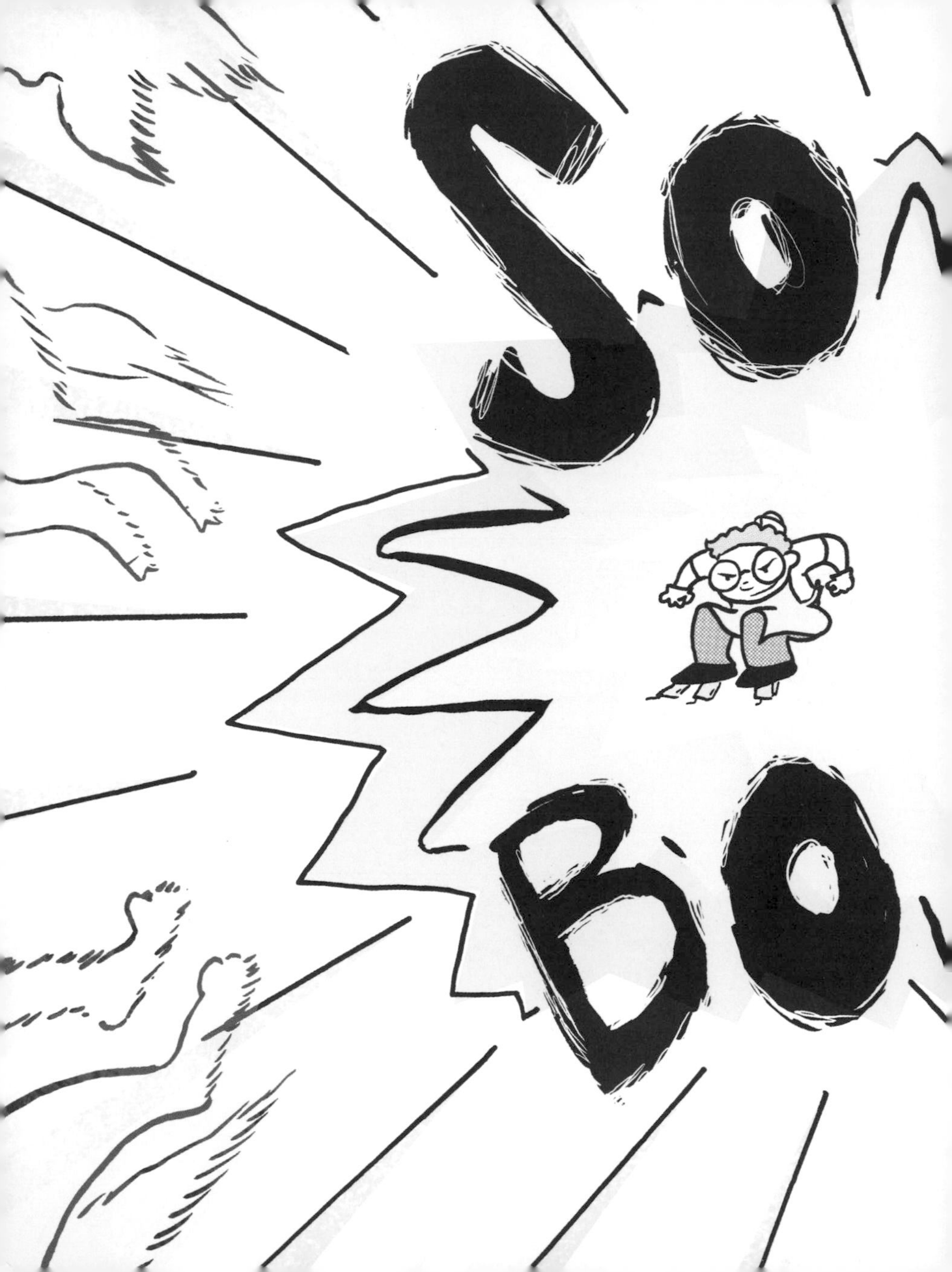
SO
BO

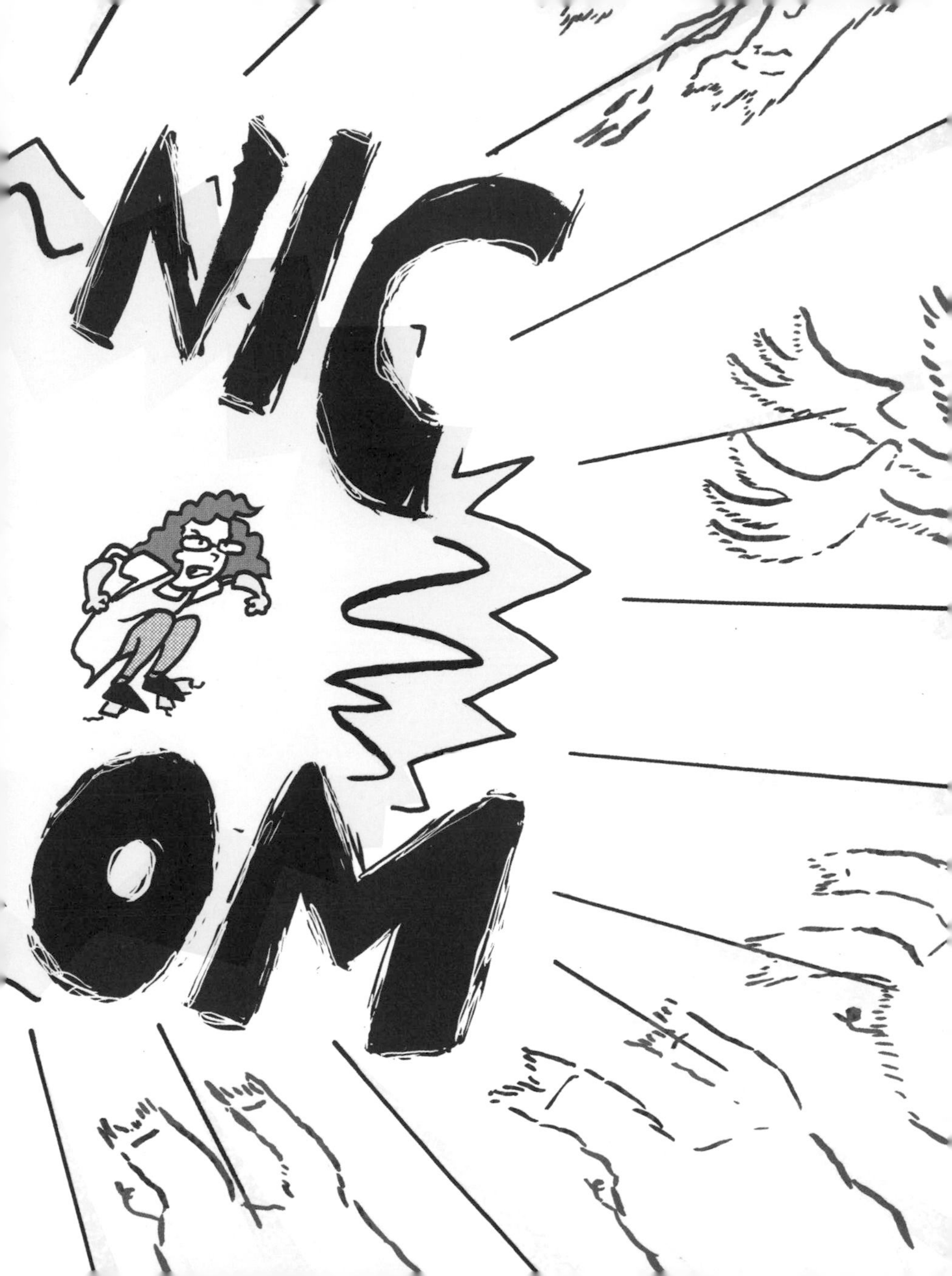

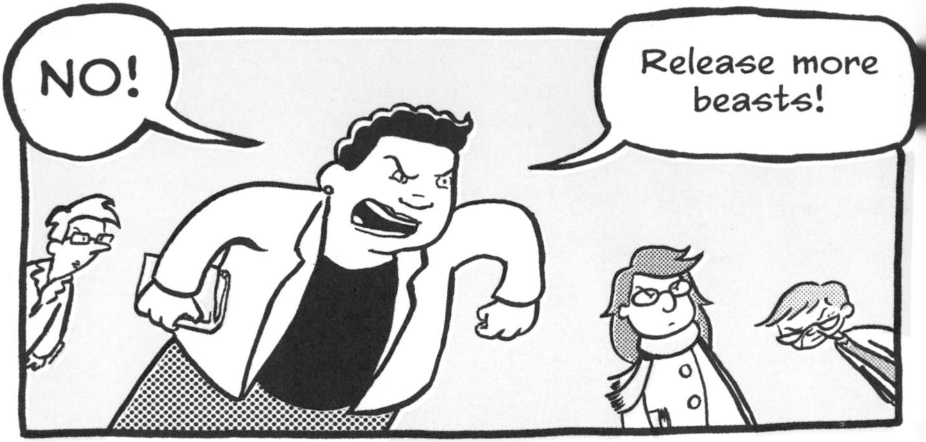
NO!
Release more beasts!

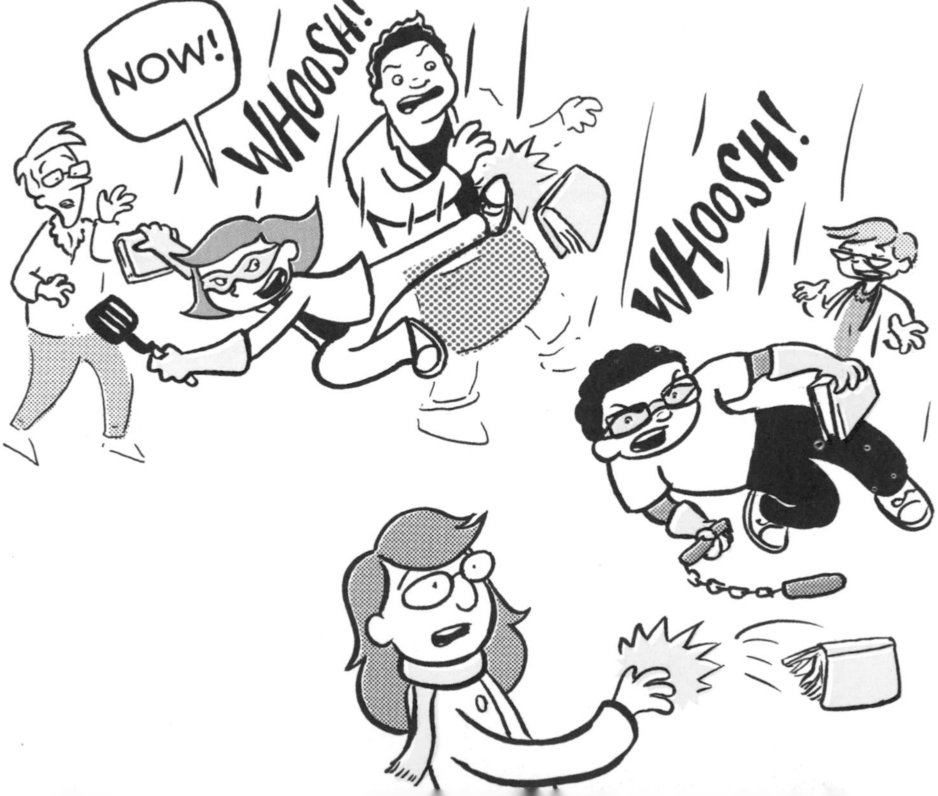
NOW!
WHOOSH!
WHOOSH!

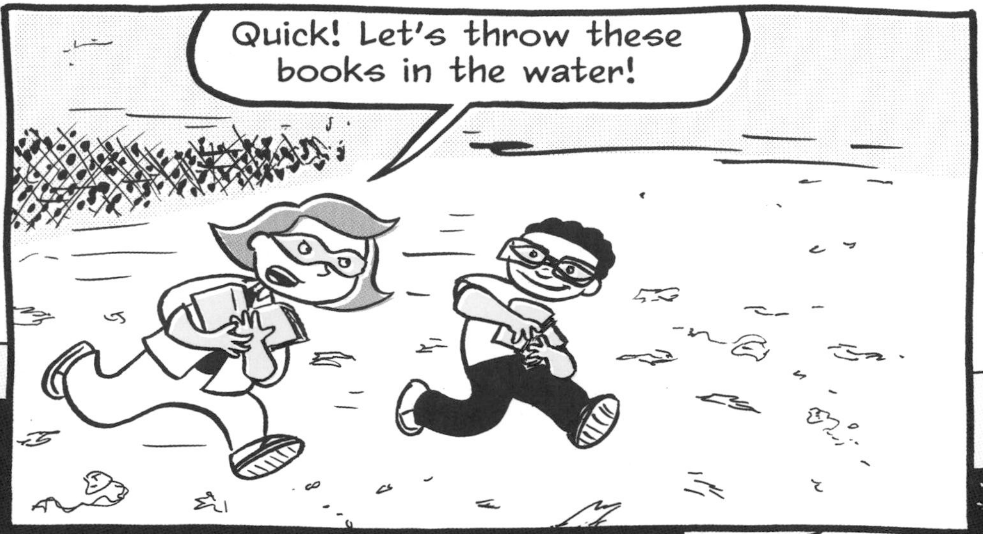
Quick! Let's throw these books in the water!

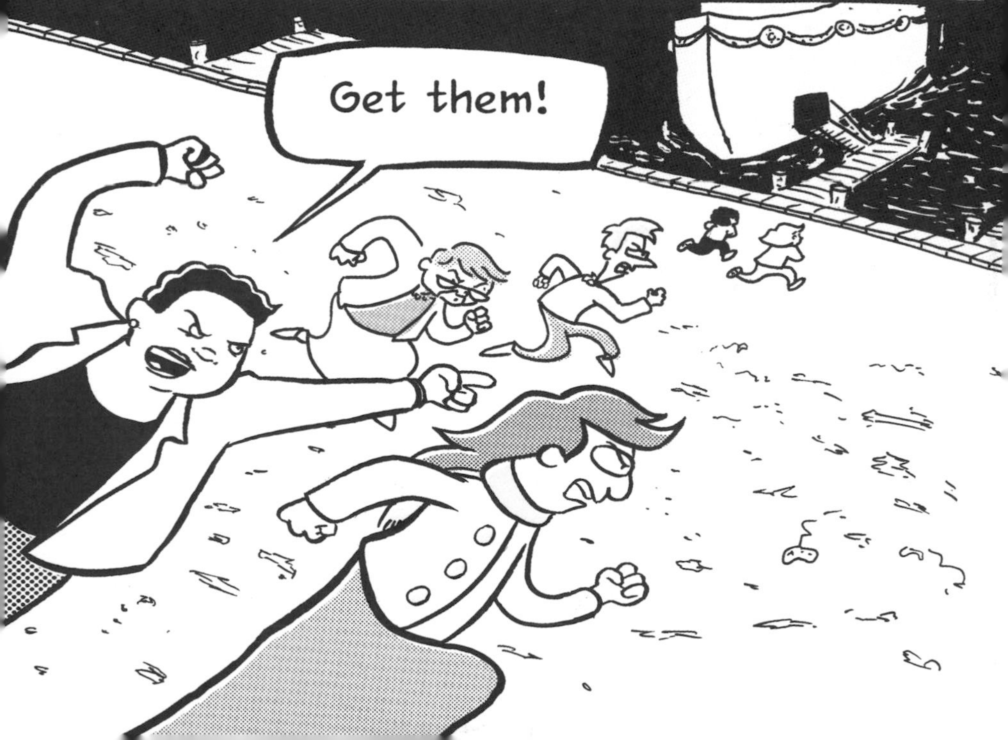
Get them!

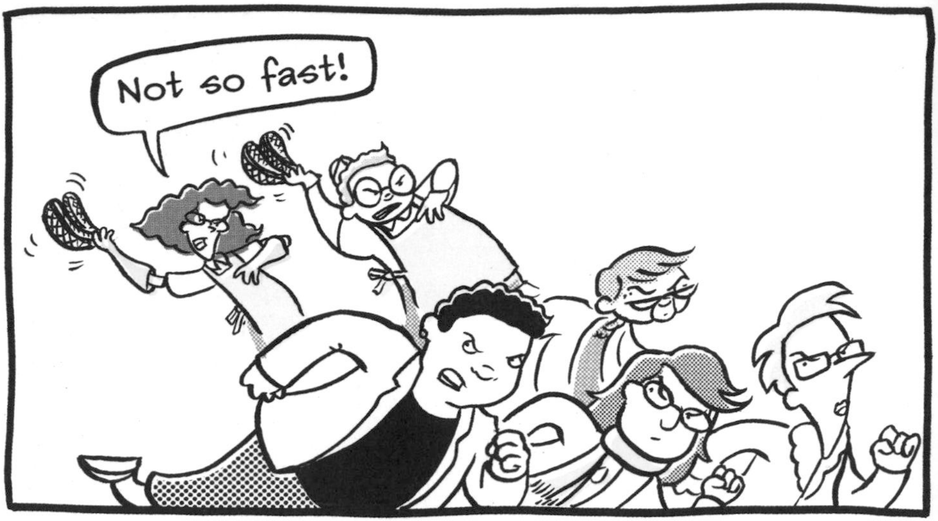
Not so fast!

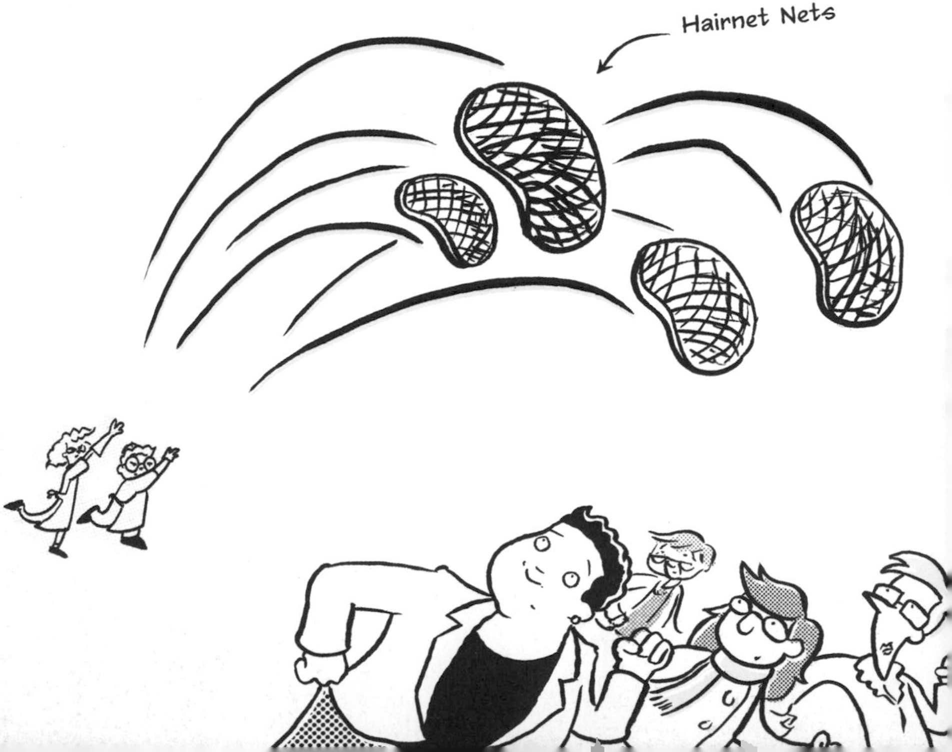
Hairnet Nets

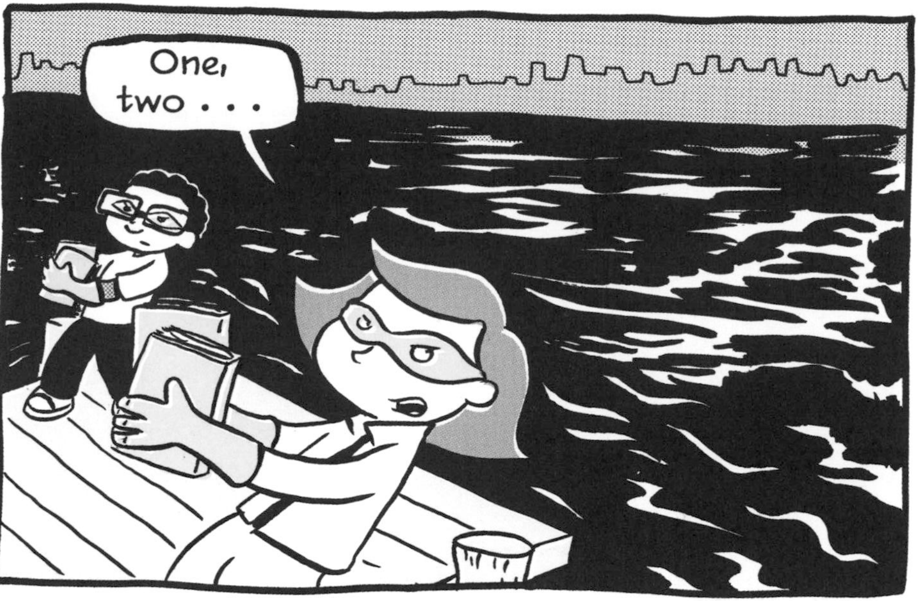
One, two . . .

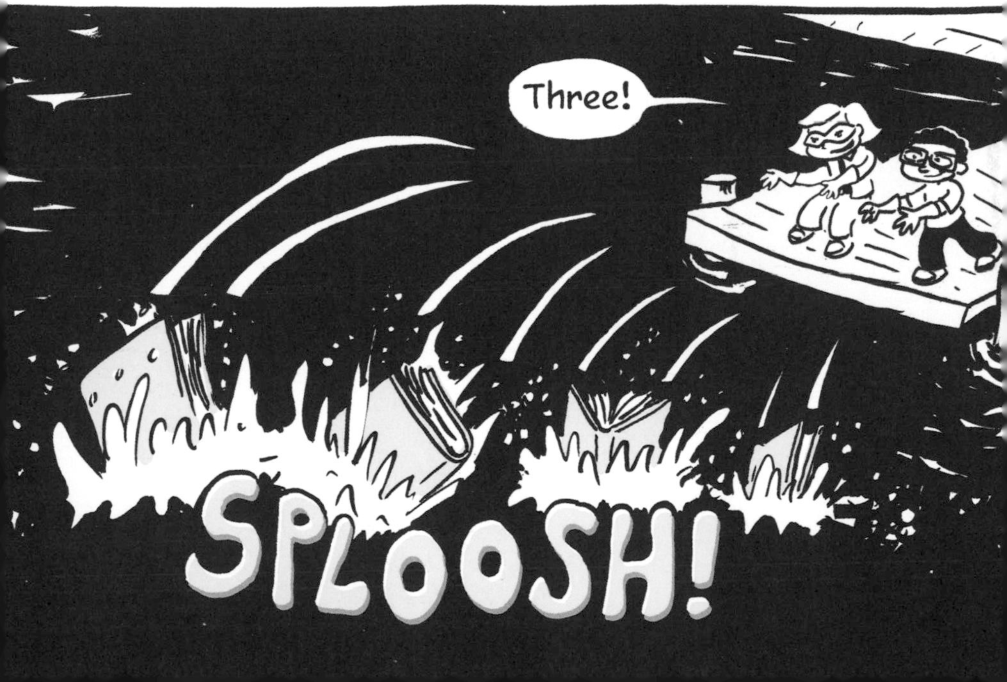
Three!
SPLOOSH!

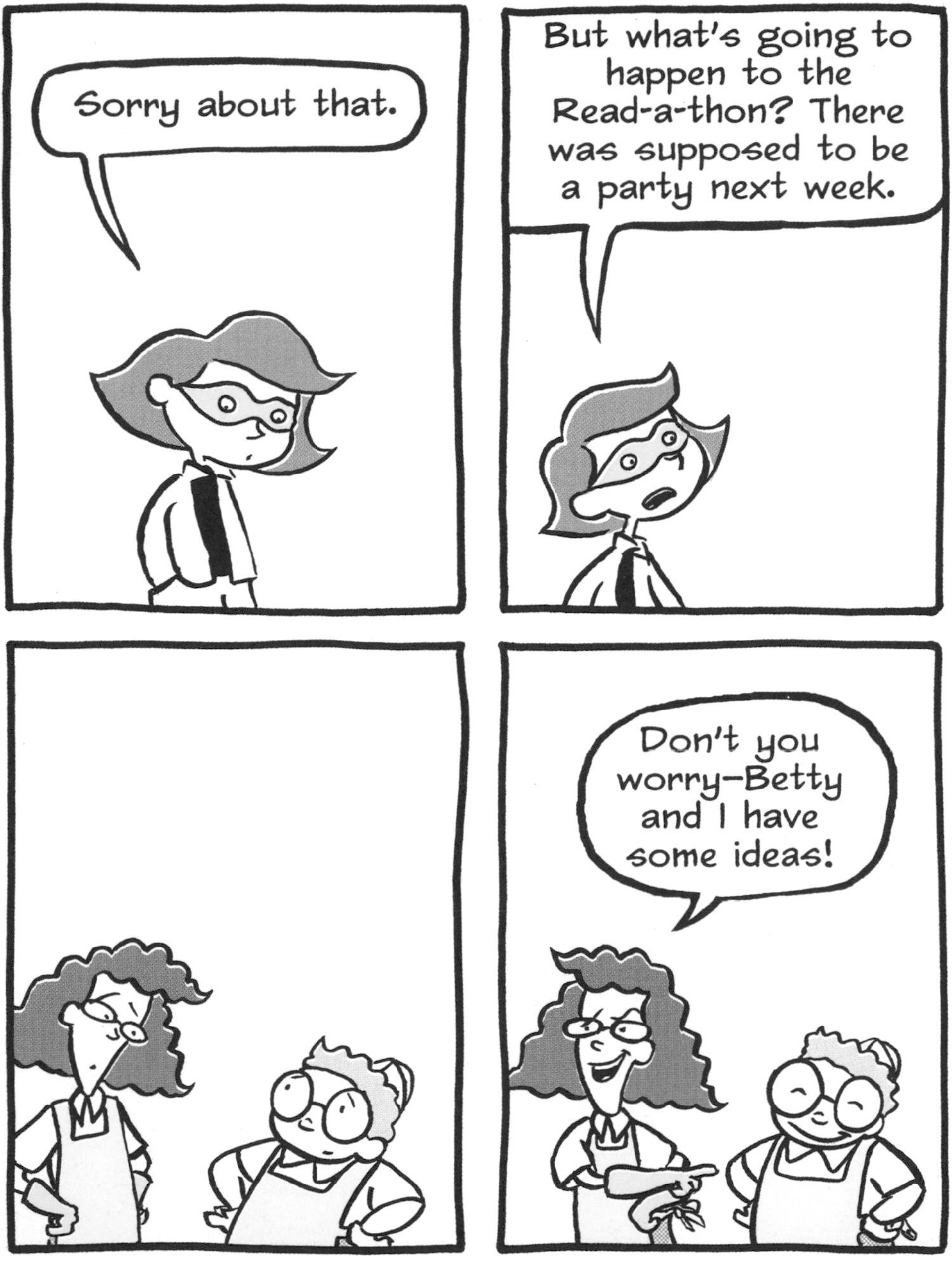
Sorry about that.
But what's going to happen to the Read-a-thon? There was supposed to be a party next week.
Don't you worry—Betty and I have some ideas!

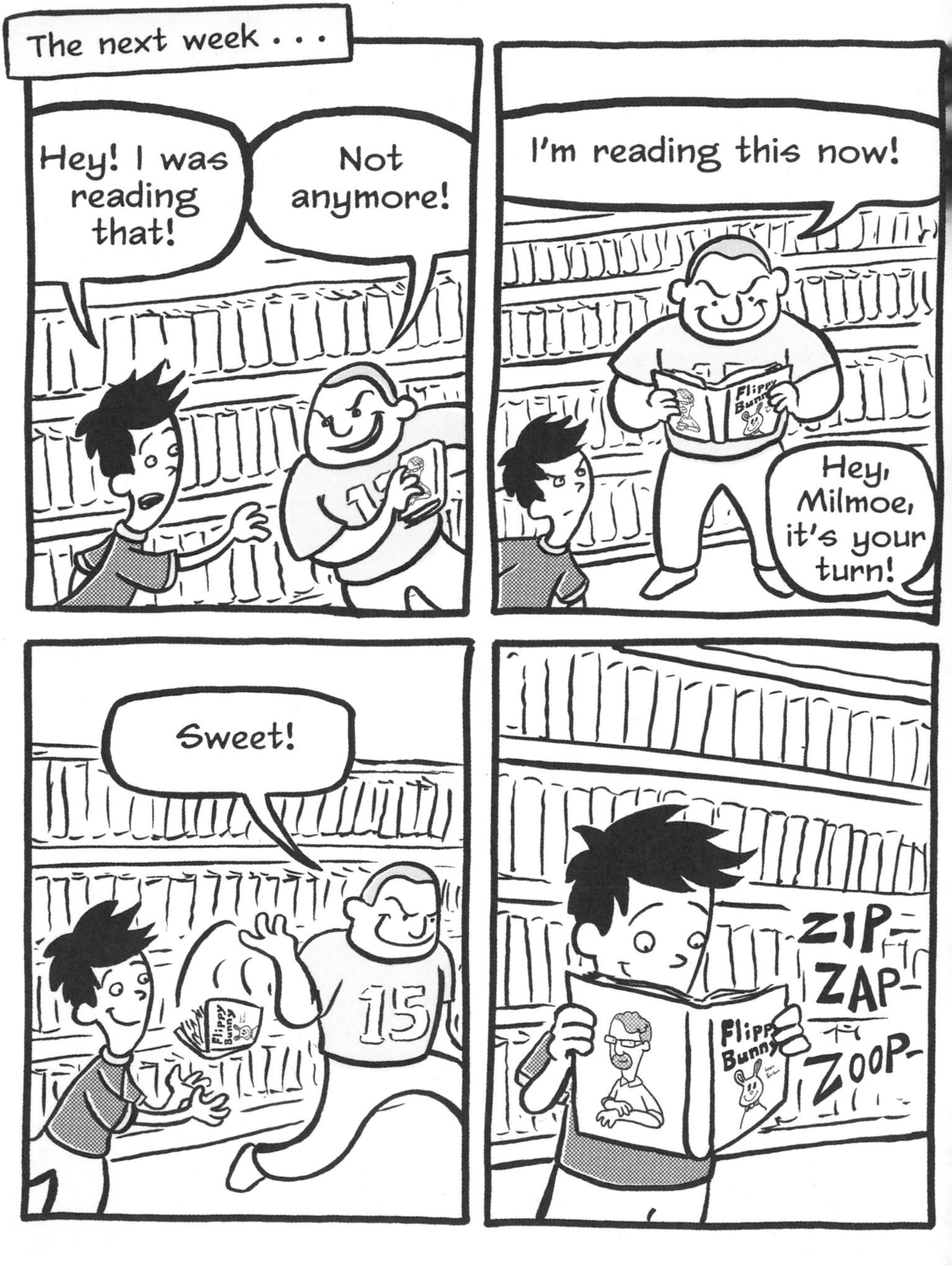
The next week . . .
Hey! I was reading that!
Not anymore!
I'm reading this now!
Flippy Bunny
Hey, Milmoe, it's your turn!
Sweet!
Flippy Bunny
15
Flippy Bunny
ZIP-
ZAP-
ZOOP-

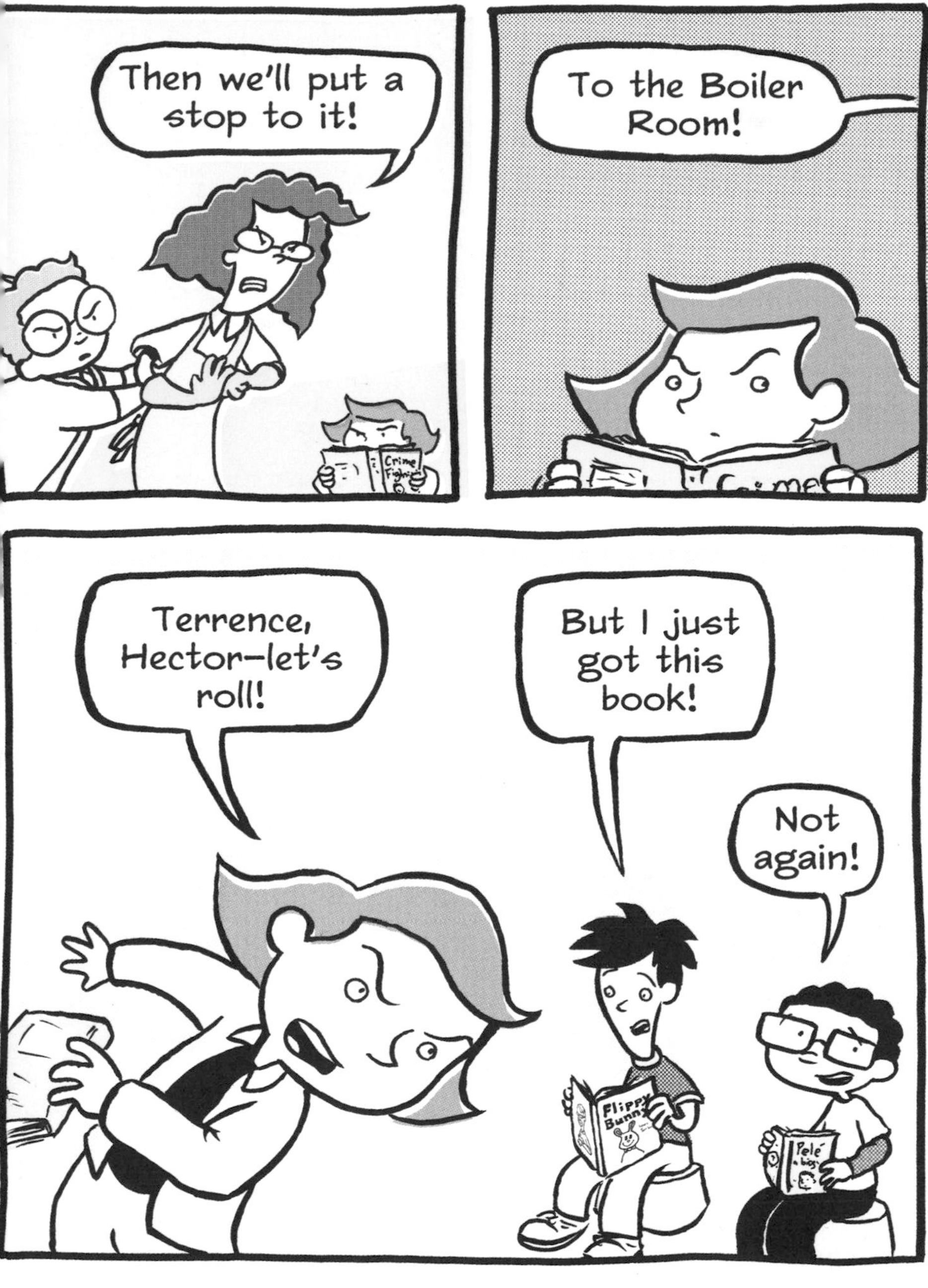
Then we'll put a stop to it!
Crime Fighting
To the Boiler Room!
Crime
Terrence, Hector—let's roll!
But I just got this book!
Not again!
Flippy Bunny
Pelé a bio

For Mrs. Krosoczka and Ralph Macchio
—J.J.K.

THIS IS A BORZOI BOOK PUBLISHED BY ALFRED A. KNOPF

All rights reserved. Published in the United States by Alfred A. Knopf, an imprint of Random House Children's Books, a division of Random House, Inc., New York.

Knopf, Borzoi Books, and the colophon are registered trademarks of Random House, Inc.

Visit us on the Web! www.randomhouse.com/kids

Educators and librarians, for a variety of teaching tools,
visit us at www.randomhouse.com/teachers

Library of Congress Cataloging-in-Publication Data
Krosoczka, Jarrett.
Lunch Lady and the League of Librarians / Jarrett J. Krosoczka. — 1st ed.
p. cm.
Summary: The school lunch lady, a secret crime fighter, sets out to stop a group
of librarians bent on destroying a shipment of video games while a group of students
known as the Breakfast Bunch provides backup.
ISBN 978-0-375-84684-7 (trade pbk.) — ISBN 978-0-375-94684-4 (lib. bdg.)
1. Graphic novels. [1. Graphic novels. 2. Librarians—Fiction. 3. Books and reading—Fiction.
4. School lunchrooms, cafeterias, etc.—Fiction. 5. Schools—Fiction.] I. Title.
PZ7.7.K76Lul 2009   [Fic]—dc22   2008043117

The text of this book is set in 11-point Hedge Backwards Lower.

MANUFACTURED IN CHINA
July 2009
20

First Edition